SEVEN LONELY CASTAWAYS

A Gilligan's Island Parody for Adults Only

J.C. Cummings

Seven Lonely Castaways
A Gilligan's Island Parody for Adults Only

© 2017 by J.C. Cummings
Tantalia Publishing
Coventry, Rhode Island U.S.A.

ISBN: 9781521155066

Cover design by VisualArts

A MESSAGE FROM J.C. CUMMINGS

Just sit right back and you'll squeeze a tail...

Ahoy, fellow lovers of all things tropical and naughty! I present to you: *Seven Lonely Castaways: A Gilligan's Island Parody for Adults Only.* This fun and steamy tale features everyone's favorite island castaways as you've *never* experienced them before! Along with Finnegan, The Captain, Mr. and Mrs. Powell, and The Doc are two of the most beautiful, sexy, and lusted-after lovelies this side of Pago Pago: Gina LaPlante and Mary Lynn Saunders, stars of every man's ultimate fantasy for over fifty years — ever since these two beauties were first marooned in TV-land and gave nearly every male on the mainland, young and old, many a rise in their Levis, along with the inspiration to begin asking that primordial question:

What *would* it be like to cuddle up with one of those gorgeous honeys in that cozy "tropic island nest" of theirs?

The debate that ensued — and continues to ensue — centers around two very obvious follow-up questions: *Which one?* and *Who's better?* Might it be Gina — the hot, voluptuous, and wanton movie star temptress? Or Mary Lynn — the sweet, innocent, and fetching farmgirl extraordinaire?

Frankly, between Gina's luscious, wide-hipped charms and Mary Lynn's sweet and tempting little curves, I simply can't decide! Therefore, I leave that decision up to you, dear reader. You will be provided with ample peeping in on each of these irresistible cuties in order to help you arrive at your own informed answers to these two oft-debated questions.

Do keep in mind, however, that your answer may very well be: "Both!"

So, what would it be like to make sweet love with either of these legendary island princesses? Well, just sit right back, read on, and you will most certainly find out. You are about to experience "tropical paradise" of a whole other order as we venture to a place where the TV cameras of yesteryear, or *any* year, were never allowed to go!

Note: before you begin, you may wish to prime both your imagination and your libido by checking out this enticing YouTube video:

https://www.youtube.com/watch?v=BCX0hov_yZQ

It features tantalizing tidbits of footage showcasing both of the original island beauties, providing you with exquisitely accurate mental pictures guaranteed to enhance your reading pleasure!

Additional note: The wording and dialogue used in this story are of the "circa-1960s-TV-land" style, in order to better recreate the true vibe of that bygone era. It may seem, at times, dated, but will help this tale to remain delightfully true to the tone of the original program from which it sprang.

Psst! One more thing: As a thank-you for purchasing this book, just email me at jc.tantalia@outlook.com and enter "book offer" in the subject line. I will send you a free PDF version of this story that uses the original character names. As per copyright law, I cannot sell this book with these names, but I can give it away. And, rest assured, I will never, ever give away or sell your email address!

Happy reading!
Love, J.C.

CHAPTER ONE

Tuesday, September 5th, 1967

It was yet another majestically beautiful evening on the island. The low-lying tropical sun now sat hunched just above the tops of the palm trees, drenching everything and everyone in the kind of ethereal golden hue that can only be found on a Pacific island paradise such as this. It lit aglow the roofs of the bamboo huts that encircled the communal clearing as well as the lush growth of the surrounding jungle. It set cool fire to the crystal-clear sea and the calm, inviting lagoon. It gave a final warm caress to the salty ocean breeze that was just now drifting in.

And it shone upon the faces of the seven stranded castaways as they sat around the outdoor bamboo dining table, chatting comfortably while sipping palm-fruit tea and finishing off the last of the decadent banana cream pies that Mary Lynn had baked for dessert. Ever since they'd found themselves shipwrecked following the storm that ravaged their three-hour Hawaiian tour three years earlier, everyone had more or less written off any hope of rescue, at least in his or her private thoughts. And the truth of the matter was this suited them just fine. Although each and every one of them missed their families and their lives back home from time to time, the allure of their tropical utopia had done a good job of convincing them that there truly was no better place on earth to be than right here.

And it was moments like this: the winding-down of another pleasant and carefree day, that helped most to foster this conviction. Indeed, even Preston Powell III had grown increasingly unfazed by the distinct possibility that he might never have an opportunity to spend any more of his millions. Though he'd never admit it aloud, he found it refreshing to live in the company of people who cared not a whit about his wealth and who loved him just for *him*.

His wife, Sweetey, was perfectly content here as well. Although she still went about her day decked out in her jewels and Parisian originals, she did so out of habit and nothing more. In fact, she'd grown to prefer spending time lying on her chaise lounge out in the warm sunshine beside her husband, chatting and sipping papaya juice, far more than her former existence of hosting or attending one stuffy social gathering after another.

The Doc was more than happy to be living the scientist's dream on an island he'd come to regard as his own private research laboratory and missing not in the least his former life back home as a university research scientist, one whose work was forever interrupted by useless meetings and PR nonsense. He now spent the majority of his days passionately searching for and studying yet another specimen of exotic plant, animal, bird, or insect to add to his bulging catalog.

For her part, Mary Lynn found life here not altogether different from that back home, what with her doing the lion's share of the cooking, hut-keeping, and gardening. Nonetheless, this island was infinitely more beautiful than any Kansas farm. And even with all her chores, the relaxed pace here left her days with plenty of free time for swimming, sunbathing, sewing, baking, and enjoying the company of her fellow castaways.

Gina had had the hardest time adjusting to her new life away from the glamor and the glory of her career as a movie star. She missed the fame and the rampant Hollywood sex dearly and had only recently come to terms with the reality that out here she was just one of the gang. Still, she found it rather refreshing to be far away from the throngs of relentless autograph hunters and the even more relentless paparazzi. Now, if she could just get herself laid, everything would be fine.

Yet, the ones who appeared the most absolutely in love with island life were the Captain and Finnegan. Though there was never a shortage of work to be done seeing to the safety and comfort of the others, they embraced life here with a zest that was downright inspiring. The Captain nearly always wore a smile—except on the rare occasion when either a monsoon or a band of headhunters happened along—and even the unending challenges wrought by being stranded on an island without even so much as running water seemed to bring him great pleasure. Finnegan, too, enjoyed helping out in any way he could every bit as much as he enjoyed his fishing, his tramps through the jungle, his butterfly collection, and his nearly nonstop eating.

No one seemed in any big hurry to be "rescued" from this life—the life of most people's dreams—anytime soon.

And why should they be? In addition to being surrounded by views that rivaled even those on Waikiki, they had a veritable ocean of fish, lobster, and seafood to enjoy, plenty of succulent mangoes, bushels of bananas, unending pineapple, and coconuts right from the tree. Furthermore, there were nuts, berries, dates, and other tropical delights, any of which could be rendered into a thousand different offerings by the women. Mary Lynn's coconut and banana cream pies were to die for and even Gina proved no stranger to whipping up something tasty whenever she wasn't sunbathing, doing her hair, or admiring her gorgeous reflection upon the placid water of the lagoon.

Frankly, between the scrumptious food, the overkill of natural beauty, the carefree (and tax-free) lifestyle, and the warm camaraderie that had developed among all of them, it was hardly surprising that each and every castaway had secretly grown thankful for the storm that had delivered them here.

Intriguingly, the Captain and Finnegan had an additional and more private reason for worshipping their new life here on this island: the women. The fact that Gina LaPlante and Mary Lynn Saunders were two amazingly beautiful young ladies was not lost on either of these two salty, sex-starved seafarers, and their very presence yielded an almost unending parade of one titillating moment after another. Gina, for instance, had no qualms about offering either man a sweet, lingering, breast-to-chest kiss whenever she needed a big favor such as having Finnegan work the pedal-powered circular fan while she cooled off on her chaise for an hour, or having the Captain build her yet another, even fancier, makeup table.

Living in such close proximity also offered both men many an opportunity to cop a succulent view or two as either woman swam, sunbathed, or simply cavorted about the clearing by the huts — Gina, typically sheathed in one of her low-cut evening dresses; Mary Lynn, in her short-shorts, tight jeans, or anything else that showed off the perfection of her farm-fresh female form. And if they were lucky, a typhoon would strike the island every so often, driving everyone to seek shelter in a tiny cave where, packed in like sardines, feminine flesh would come up against male hardness every time anyone so much as inhaled.

Indeed, hardly a day went by during which the Captain and Finnegan weren't secretly thanking their lucky stars to have been marooned with the likes of Gina and Mary Lynn, no matter how chronically hard and horny it made them — nor how blue their balls.

* * * *

Later that night, while snoring in his hammock, the Captain was roused awake by faint moans and a rhythmic rustling sound from above. It didn't take him long to realize that Finnegan was at it again: stroking his ding-dong right there in his hammock.

He sighed and shook his head. So, what else was new?

"Finnegan."

No reply.

"Finnegan."

Continued moaning.

"Finnegan!"

"Um—uh—yeah, Cap'n?"

"Would you mind going out into the jungle to do that?"

The rustling stopped. "Sorry, Cap. But I just can't help myself sometimes. Besides, it's dark out there."

"Of course it's dark, you knucklehead! But, for goodness' sake, you're right on top of me!" He shook his head and sighed. "You are one horny fella, you know that? I still say it wouldn't surprise me one bit if it turned out you bungled all our rescue attempts on purpose just so you could stay here with the hopes of banging one of the girls...like that's ever going to happen."

Finnegan groaned. "Jeez, not that again. Listen, Cap, you're right...I probably don't have a chance with either Gina or Mary Lynn. So, why would I bungle rescues when there are plenty of chicks in Honolulu I *could* score with? Besides, I haven't seen you or anyone else on this island building any rescue rafts or signal towers lately. Face it: we're happy here." He zipped his sailor pants back up. "Anyway, I'm sorry for doing it right on top of you. It's just hard—"

"Seems to me it's *hard* all the time," the Captain interrupted, chuckling.

Finnegan offered a cynical laugh in return. "Look who's talking."

"You got me there, little buddy. Yes, I do know where you're coming from on that score."

"Yeah," his first mate answered. "I'm *coming* from right above you!"

The two shared another laugh at that one.

Then, seconds later: "So, which one were you thinking about this time?"

A pause. "Both, actually."

"Both, huh?" The Captain smiled and yawned. "Hm, been there more than a few times myself."

"Yeah," Finnegan went on, his voice now dripping with testosterone, "I was thinking about what it would be like for Gina and Mary Lynn to be going at it out by the lagoon or maybe in their hut. *Mmm*...rubbing warm coconut oil all over each other and letting it trickle across each other's titties...and then rubbing 'em against each other. Imagine that, Cap! Gina's jugs and Mary Lynn's mamas just slipping and sliding all over the place? *Ooh!* And then they could start licking it off each other's—"

"All right, Finnegan, stop! Now you're getting me worked up, too!"

"Can't help it, Cap. I just can't stop thinking about Gina showing Mary Lynn how to *really* have some fun with that coconut oil, y'know what I'm

16

saying? And—*ahhh*—imagine Gina rubbing some of that stuff all over Mary Lynn's *ass*!" A pause. "Man, wouldn't *that* be a sight? A butt as gorgeous as Mary Lynn's...all slippery and warm and—*unhh*—so gorgeous!"

"I'm right with you on that one, too," the Captain acknowledged. "Our little Mary Lynn definitely has a booty to beat the band. Whenever she walks around in those short shorts of hers, I can't take my eyes off it. It's cute...it's curvy..." Another yawn. "It's perfect."

"It's *better* than perfect," Finnegan countered. "Not that Gina isn't built nice, too."

"You don't have to remind me of *that*!" The Captain shifted his weight more comfortably in his hammock. "Do you realize how lucky we are, Finnegan? Not only do we have an actual movie star living with us—a gorgeous movie star to boot—but one who's always dressing those curves of hers in those tight dresses and wiggling her hips like a pair of windshield wipers everywhere she goes."

"And don't forget the waterfall."

"Oh, my gosh, never! I mean, wasn't that the most incredible thing you ever saw? What a sight! Gina LaPlante...showering nude under a tropical waterfall! I'll tell you, I couldn't get enough of those breasts of hers! And those legs! I mean, her thighs just went on forever!" He shook his head in amazement. "If we ever found a way to ferry men over here from Honolulu, we could make a killing charging admission to *that* show!"

He daydreamed on that enticing venture for a moment, then continued. "Anyway, I still can't believe it took us until now to even think about taking a peek at her. If you hadn't been out butterfly hunting with my binoculars the other day…"

Finnegan laughed quietly. "Come on, Cap. Do you actually believe I was out looking for freaking butterflies? Or that I *came across* her by accident? Jesus, give me a little credit. It took me over an hour just to find the perfect peeping spot, for chrissake."

The Captain sighed again. "Like I said: one horny fella."

Finnegan leaned over and looked him in the eye. "I didn't exactly have to twist *your* arm to come with me the last couple of times, though, did I? Come on, admit it, Cap. *Sometimes* I do something right."

The Captain laughed. "All right, little buddy, I'll grant you that. You definitely made up for a whole lot of foul-ups with that one. Thanks to you, we even know she's a natural redhead."

Finnegan snickered, then lay back down. "Thanks to your binoculars, too. Man, I could even make out the goosebumps on her nips with those babies."

To which the Captain found himself reaching for his own mast, squeezing it hard at the memory of Gina soaping up her absolutely stunning knockers. Never in his life had he ever seen a more perfect pair on a woman. He could just imagine her world-famous flesh filling his hands...all sudsy and slippery.

Just then, Finnegan's voice broke his lusty train of thought. "Hey, Cap? Who do you think is hotter anyway? Gina? Or Mary Lynn?"

The Captain pursed his lips as he gripped his little first mate more tightly and gave the matter serious thought.

He recalled the time, two years earlier, when Gina and Mary Lynn had had that nasty fight over Gina's unwillingness to do her share of the chores. Gina had stormed off and built her own little hovel of a hut and then...the first strong wind to come along that night and, boom, down it went. And there was Gina, racing from the pile of bamboo and palm fronds straight to their front door, wearing nothing but her very sheer, very well-filled bra and lacy pink panties. She was hysterical, of course, and not quite aware of the fact that, during her five-minute tirade, he and Finnegan had allowed their eyes, and their very dirty minds, to have their way with her mango-sized mammaries and their clearly defined tasty-buds. Conveniently, she was also oblivious to the blatant bulges her semi-clad arrival had elicited in their pants.

Then he thought about the time last year when that monsoon had swept in without warning. Everyone else had already raced for cover in the cave when he suddenly realized that Mary Lynn was missing. He'd raced off into the jungle to search for her and found her stuck in the mud bog she'd been relaxing in. There she was, in up to her neck and panicked beyond all get-out. Thinking fast, he heaved and pulled and out she popped wearing nothing but a tempting layer of mud and the most embarrassed look of gratitude he'd ever seen. Sure, she immediately snatched up her clothes to throw on, but still, during those few seconds in between, the rain washed no small amount of mud away and mmm, boy, were those gorgeous cheeks of hers a sight! It was all he could think about for the rest of the day.

"Well?" Finnegan urged. "Come on, which one?"

"Well, little buddy, I guess it comes down to a toss-up between Gina's boobs and Mary Lynn's butt." He shrugged. "So, I guess it depends on whether either one is coming or going. What about you?"

Finnegan gave a short laugh. Then, his voice matter-of-fact, he replied, "Coming, going, tits, ass, day, night, inside-out, or upside-down. I'd take either one seven ways from Sunday, Cap. Makes no difference to me."

The Captain gave a final yawn and closed his eyes once again. "Yup, one horny fella..." he mumbled just before falling back to sleep, his dreams now centered upon Gina's world-class 36 double-D's and Mary Lynn's delectable derriere.

Intriguingly, the Captain and Finnegan weren't the only ones thinking unwholesome thoughts about their foxy female fellow castaways that night...

* * * *

In the next hut, the Doc was hunched over his table, busily writing in his journal by the light of a trio of candles. He'd been religiously filling the massive homemade volume for over a year now, ever since he'd figured out how to make paper from native hemp. The leather cover was fashioned from the skin of a wild boar they'd captured and butchered around that same time and his pen was made from whittled koa wood filled with octopus ink. The journal was divided into two sections. The first was his science journal, which was primarily a detailed catalog of every species of plant and animal he'd researched here on the island. The second was his personal diary, which included both a chronicle of their many shared adventures here as well as a collection of philosophical musings and essays.

And it was one of these: an essay on the subject of sexuality and forced isolation—more specifically, Gina and Mary Lynn—that occupied his pen hand at the moment.

What inexplicable and fascinating power has worked its way into the libidos of the Captain and Finnegan over the course of our thirty-six months here on the island! It is plain to see their raised eyebrows and craning necks whenever one of the women passes by or is seen in some compromising pose or another. And, all too often, I've witnessed the risings of their male organs that typically result.

I personally have never held the slightest interest in lusting after members of the opposite sex, engrossed as I am wont to be in my many studies on chemistry and biology. Yet, in recent weeks, I must confess that the increasing attention placed on the physical attributes of Gina and Mary Lynn by the other men—even Mr. Powell—has caused my own thoughts to stray in a new and rather carnal direction. I've even caught myself gazing secretively upon the physiques of both women, which, more often than not, has resulted in very distracting churnings in my own loins as well.

I find the whole matter rather disturbing.

And, for reasons I can't explain, quite stimulating as well. Gina's well-endowed bosom has become a most compelling distraction and I frequently find myself trying to imagine what her breasts must look like unclothed: their shape, their softness, their nipples, and, more enticing still, what they might feel like within my hands. I will never have the opportunity for such an experience, of course. Nonetheless, I am now certain it would have been a most gratifying delight.

Then there is the matter of Mary Lynn. It now seems that every time she passes by I find myself turning to behold her gently swaying hips and splendid gluteus maximus. I must say, I've never held much of an interest in geometry, yet the shape and curvature of her rear quarters have had a profound impact on my thoughts as well as a greatly increased flow of blood to my male organ. I can only imagine how wonderful her well-shaped flesh would feel — so soft, smooth, and supple — though, again, I am certain I will never have the opportunity to prove or disprove that assumption.

In any event, if I am to continue my research cataloging the multitude of tropical flora and fauna here, I need a clear head. The prospect of presenting a comprehensive study on the indigenous life-forms on this island to the scientific community (if we are ever rescued) is far too important an opportunity to miss. It would certainly be a feather in my cap and earn me much respect from my peers.

Given the importance of my work, I thus cannot afford to be consumed by my sexual longings any longer. Indeed, I must take every measure I can to curb my nascent libido and put an end to this uncomfortable distraction, pleasurable though it may be.

The Doc lowered his pen and looked out through the window into the night. "Perhaps," he mused, "through grit, determination and sheer force of will, if I were to focus *all* of my attention and energy solely upon my work…"

He closed and reopened his journal to the science section, then flipped through the pages to his most recent entry: a comprehensive detailing of the courtship habits of the Mynah bird. But no sooner had he begun to read and revise, his mind became filled once again with thoughts of Gina: his fingers moving across her voluptuous breasts…squeezing them…tasting them…and then of Mary Lynn: his hands exploring her wondrous behind…caressing it…fondling it…

The Doc looked down at his quickly stiffening male organ and released a long, sad sigh, shaking his head in abject disappointment.

Apparently, force of will would not suffice in this matter.

He moaned in discouragement, then closed the journal. "Tomorrow," he said with quiet determination, "efforts will, indeed, be redoubled."

CHAPTER TWO

Meanwhile, on an island many miles to the south...

The Palace of the Gods sat upon the highest promontory on the grand isle of Tiazanu, overlooking the darkened ocean. Fashioned from bamboo, teak, and cut stone; lit by the flames of a thousand tiki torches, it was an indoor-outdoor royal sanctuary like no other in the entire Sea of Ever-Peace. Its sheer size and majesty commanded respect and awe from all of the island's inhabitants, as did the King of Tiazanu himself, a leader who was at once revered for his kindness and feared for his fierce temper.

And, as was known to all, this was a palace within which much more than royal administration and decree took place...

From atop his throne of bamboo and silk, King Palawani moved his gaze away from the crashing waves far below and down upon his young nude concubine, Kili-anu, as she zestfully performed his evening servicing. He frowned and shook his head. It wasn't working tonight. Enticingly beautiful, nubile, and skillful though she was, he simply could not...could not...could not arrive at his ultimate release. It mattered not how swiftly her lips worked, nor the way in which she slid her small breasts, firm as papayas, up and down and across his thighs.

Sadly, he'd suffered the same disappointment the night before as well. Truth be told, he had not experienced full release for nearly an entire moon cycle now; not with Kili-anu, nor with any of his five others. Even Miawanini, his oldest and most skilled mistress, with her strong musculature and wealth of experience, could no longer bring him to the loftiest peaks of male enlightenment as she once had.

No, none of his mistresses appeared capable of satisfying his needs anymore. And, curse the gods, if he only knew why! They were certainly beautiful. As king of Tiazanu, it was his royal privilege to select only the most alluring maidens from throughout the isle. Only those with the most angelic faces, comely figures, and youthful exuberance were invited to live lives of luxury and comfort here in his royal compound. Certainly, he had chosen well, for all six were unquestionably alluring and their womanly adornments well-formed by the gods. Furthermore, every one of them had been thoroughly schooled in the art of male pleasure by his second senior mistress, Kalali. They were certainly as capable as they were beautiful.

And yet, it was now painfully apparent that their beauty and skill were no longer sufficient, for, once again, his evening session was leaving him woefully incapable of expelling his kingly seed. It would, of course, have been easy to place the blame on Kili-anu and the others and thus remain above judgment. But he knew all too well that the fault was not theirs, for what they did had once sufficed and yet now it did not. He knew that the blame lay within him and, most embarrassingly, he was certain that they knew it as well.

King Palawani was, indeed, confused and ashamed.

He sighed, shook his head, then gently pulled Kili-anu from his loins. Then he carefully rearranged his grass skirt to cover his Royal Limpness.

"Pulu si bagumba, laloli. Tikiki ho-hopu kata-ramu," he said wearily. *That is enough, my mistress. Return to your chamber.*

Kili-anu looked up at him, her opal eyes now filled with fear. "Despite my most sincere effort, I have once again failed to bring My King to fulfillment." She swallowed and lowered her eyes once again. "Am I...to be fed to the God of Death-Lava?"

He sighed and trailed his fingers through her long, straight, black hair. Then he shook his head and signaled for her to rise.

"No. You have done your utmost and I am most impressed and pleasured by your efforts. I am certain it is the God of Man-Joy who is withholding my fulfillment—for what reason, I do not know. Alas, the gods do work in mysterious ways. In any event, the fault is not yours. It is a matter which I and I alone must resolve. Meanwhile, you may go."

Kili-anu smiled faintly and bowed. "Many thanks, My King." She started to leave, then stopped and returned to his side. Inhaling deeply, she lowered herself across his plump lap, presenting him with her pleasant little curves. "Would it please My King to administer a spanking before I leave, as a reminder for me to render my services more skillfully from now on?"

King Palawani gazed upon her lovely pose, stroked her firm flesh gently, and pursed his lips. "Your offer is most gracious and tempting, my mistress. But, as you are aware, I have much to think about at present. Perhaps later."

Kili-anu stood, bowed once again, and left the Grand Overlook, her movements alluring as always, despite her now woeful countenance.

The king sighed once again as he watched her walk away. Such a beautiful young woman. Beautiful and talented. In days' past, even with such a simple act as walking, she could bring his Royal Scepter to the ready. But now—he looked down upon his dormant loins—even this was becoming a rarity.

What was it? What was wrong? Why were his mistresses no longer capable of providing him complete fulfillment? If it were not a matter of allure, nor a matter of expertise, nor a matter of effort, what, then, could it possibly be?

He thought of each in turn: Kili-anu, Midori, Miawanini, Kalali, Pua-nua, Katata—all with their strikingly long, straight, black hair and their smooth skin the color of koa wood—all with their trim, youthful hips, pert breasts, and shapely thighs. Every mistress was exquisite. Every one of them was of the highest quality. Every one of them was…

He stopped and looked out across the moonlit oceanic view before him, thinking.

Then, after the arrival of many waves, it came to him. Every one of them was…

The same.

He nodded assuredly. That was it! For all their unparalleled beauty, his fabulous mistresses were all very much the same. Same in shape. Same in skin. Same in face. Furthermore, same in their capabilities and same in their offerings.

Yes, that was it. Every erotic pleasure he received from every mistress was, in fact, the very same pleasure.

And, thus, every day had now become the very same day.

He nodded again, this time with utter conviction, for he had at last determined the cause of his shortcoming.

But, as for a solution, he had no answers.

Perhaps this was a matter beyond his own ability to remedy. Perhaps it was time to seek the assistance of his advisor, Jia-banu.

The wisest and most revered woman on the island. She would certainly be able to provide him with the wisdom and advice he needed.

He smiled, picked up his royal conch shell, and blew thrice.

* * * *

Early the next morning, following a night of one curve-filled dream after another, the Doc woke with renewed determination to put an end to his runaway male urges. Before he could talk himself out of it, he got out of bed, donned a pair of shorts and sneakers, and then set off on a good hard three laps around the southern half of the island. He knew that heavy exercise was very effective in calming sexual urges, so although he was not one for athletics, he called upon every ounce of willpower and energy he had and, by the start of his second lap, his broad chest and back were coated with a sheen of perspiration.

Nonetheless, it felt good to be expending this much energy, free from the grasp of his licentious longings.

Unfortunately, by the time he passed through the clearing a second time, the women were outside, setting the table for breakfast. There was Gina, in her low-cut pink dress, brazenly presenting her deep, swaying cleavage as she set out a bowl of fruit. And there was Mary Lynn, wearing her tight white jeans and providing him with a good long look at her stunning backside as she bent down to tend to a pan of breadfruit pancakes on the fire.

Their own surprised and appreciative glances at his bare-chested body as he ran past were equally distracting.

Three seconds later, he looked back over his shoulder for one more peek...

Two seconds after that he ran straight into a palmetto bush.

So much for exercise.

Still determined, the Doc spent the rest of the morning searching for an assortment of jungle plants with which to brew a potion that was sure to curb his penile pulsations.

But even after downing two cups of the horrid tasting concoction, he realized just how ineffective it was when, not an hour later, he spotted Mary Lynn out behind her hut, hanging her clothes and pretty underwear out to dry, stretching *way* up in those altogether too-tight jeans and her tightly-tucked yellow blouse.

He very nearly moistened his shorts right then and there.

And then, late in the afternoon, as he knelt to start the evening fire, Gina came sauntering into the clearing wearing her leopard bikini and walked straight up to him, swinging her hips wide and smooth as ever.

"Doc, I just wanted to thank you for that new batch of suntan lotion you made." She bent down and planted a lingering, moist kiss on his quickly overwhelmed lips. "I had it on all afternoon while I was sunning myself at the lagoon. It felt so nice on my skin and, see? I didn't burn at all!" His eyes followed her fingertips as they trailed up and down her tanned thigh, then across the tops of her breasts. "Mmm, smells wonderful, too, don't you think?" She passed her wrist beneath his nose, then straightened.

"Oh, um, it was n-no problem at all, Gina," he replied awkwardly, his eyes now finding themselves at the same height as her reproductive region. "New, um, formula. And I added a mixture of hibiscus, orchid, and jasmine extracts for fragrance."

"Well, you sure are a smart man, Doc," she said admiringly. "Thanks again." She placed another kiss on his cheek, then, after brushing her semi-naked hip lightly against his shoulder, she turned and went inside her hut.

He was now highly aware of the tingles on his cheek and lips as well as the tightening of his trousers as his watched her sashay away.

Dinner was no better. Every time Mary Lynn so much as moved he found himself mesmerized by the beauty of her face and hair, the allure of her glistening lips as she spoke, and the tantalizing line of her thighs as she sat, legs crossed, in those amazing little short-shorts of hers. He found it nearly impossible to keep his eyes off her. Nothing she said or did would have been regarded by anyone as 'arousing,' yet everything she did was thoroughly arousing simply because it was *her* doing it. Why, she could simply pass him the bowl of guava jelly, tilt her head, smile sweetly, and he would scarcely even taste the stuff.

Then Gina had to get him and everyone else going with yet another story of a naked weekend she'd spent at Lake Tahoe, in the vacation home of a Hollywood producer. She left out no detail regarding the hot tub, the champagne, the French maid costume, or the bearskin rug in front of the fireplace — every one explicit enough to conjure up a collage of images in his mind that were downright pornographic.

I'm doomed, he repeated silently to himself, for not the last time.

That night, as he wrote of the day's disappointments in his diary, he came to the conclusion that this problem had become bigger than his ability to control it, and the lapse in his research on the Mynah bird was proof. He couldn't get his mind off Gina or Mary Lynn no matter what he did or how hard he tried.

He sighed sadly as he continued with his discouraging entry.

Then, seemingly out of nowhere, the wise words of Carl Jung arose in his thoughts:

What we resist, persists.

What we accept, lightens.

Yes, brilliant man, Jung was.

Right then, the Doc made a decision: He would place his current scientific work on hold for the time being, yield to the power of his persistent inner urges, and devote himself entirely to the deep study of this other, more relevant branch of biology: male sexuality.

Namely: his.

After all, he was a scientist, for goodness' sake. His curious and active mind needed stimulation; he needed to study *something*. Therefore, why not study that which he seemed most drawn to at the present time? Truth be told, he found this subject to be curiously more compelling than the study of Mynah birds. So, why not put his six degrees and keen intellect to more personally gratifying use?

Having no experience whatsoever in this realm meant that there was much to learn and he found himself strangely eager to get started.

But what hypothesis might he build his study around? What, specifically, should he study?

For several minutes, the Doc thought hard on the matter.

Then, taking a deep breath, he flipped to a fresh new page in the science section of his journal and divided it into two columns. At the top of the left column, he printed "Gina" and at the top of the right column, "Mary Lynn." On the facing page, he wrote out the primary thesis question to be explored:

Which beautiful castaway possesses the superior female anatomy, the highest degree of beauty, the most alluring ambiance, and, thus, the greater ability to attract and arouse a man?

In layman's terms: Who would offer the most sexual gratification?

Or, even more succinctly: Who was better?

Gina?

Or Mary Lynn?

The Doc looked down at the page, his mind spinning off in a dozen different and titillating directions.

He smiled broadly. This was sure to be his most gratifying study to date.

* * * *

Over the course of the next two days, the Doc kept a close and very grateful eye on both women in an effort to gather as much data as possible. As always, each one offered no small number of viewing opportunities, as the typically sultry tropical sunshine kept them in revealing attire from dawn to dusk. Gina usually preferred one of her several shape-defining dresses that showcased her beautiful bosom marvelously and hugged her wide, curvaceous hips with perfection. On one particularly warm day, she opted for a colorful wraparound skirt and matching bikini top which, as always, brought open-mouthed stares from the other men, even Mr. Powell, for which he received a hard slap on the arm from Mrs. Powell. Gina knew they were staring, of course. He could tell by the faint knowing smile she wore whenever they were in her presence, and by the extra wide arc that she would add to the swing of her hips whenever she passed by.

What she didn't know was that *he* was now drinking in the sight of her world-renowned architecture every bit as much as the others. He was careful not to allow his peeping to become noticeable, and he was certain she had no inkling whatsoever of the fact that he was now frequently undressing her with his eyes, imagining himself gently freeing her heavy breasts from her bikini top, unwrapping that sheer skirt, and sliding her panties down her long, luscious legs...

After all, he needed a comprehensive supply of data in order for his study to remain credible and ultimately conclusive. Thus, it was imperative that he pay close attention to every inch of every curve she had. In the name of science, he needed to accurately estimate the firmness of her breasts, along with such ancillary factors as possible nipple placement, the hue of her areoles, and overall jiggle quotient. He needed to speculate on the tone and spreadability of her thighs and what they might feel like wrapped around a man. He needed to think long and hard on what if would feel like to place his hands upon her wide hips as he entered her.

All findings were painstakingly recorded in page after page of his increasingly salacious journal.

Then there was Mary Lynn, coming and going throughout her day wearing either her girl-next-door red gingham dress, her denim short-shorts and orange halter top, or any of her pairs of jeans that simply molded themselves to her curves. He was soon convinced that there wasn't a woman on earth who could wear jeans quite like her. No one but Mary Lynn could possibly fill them out with as much artistry as she. He pictured himself kneeling before her, then slowly unzipping and pulling down those jeans to reveal pretty white satiny panties. He was certain they would feel beyond exquisite as he caressed her through them and cupped her bottom. Next, he would slip one hand down beneath the waistband and the other hand up inside the leg openings. He would groan and she would gasp as his fingers made contact with, he was certain, her hitherto untouched womanly recess...

Yes, in order to bolster the accuracy of his visualizations, he needed to keep a close eye on Mary Lynn as well. He needed to catalog every tight contour she had. He needed to observe with a keen eye her slim bare waist and wonder if it would be possible to encircle it entirely within his hands. He needed to speculate on how tight the back pockets of her jeans would feel if he were to slide his fingers inside them. He needed to imagine her lying on her side on a soft bed, completely undressed, looking both shy and wanton as he came to her, her lips and tongue glistening in the moonlight.

Yes, he needed to amass a veritable mountain of data in order for this project to succeed—mounds and mounds of it. And that data was not confined merely to each woman's primary sex characteristics; those with headings such as "Breasts," "Lips, "Legs," "Hips," or "Gluteus Maximus." Given his penchant for thoroughness, the Doc also included such sub-headings as: "Smile," "Earlobes," "Hair," "Eyes," "Tongue," "Voice," and "Stride." Indeed, any aspect of their being which might enhance or contribute to each woman's capacity to allure was carefully notated.

Additionally, both women also offered up plenty of accidental, yet provocative, poses for his eyes to examine and his mind to speculate on. There were always clothes to be hung, the table to be bent over while setting out a freshly-baked pie, low-lying flowers to be picked, high-hanging mangoes to be reached for, chaises to be lounged upon, and, of course, sun-rays to be worshiped.

Likewise, there were plenty of opportunities for a bit of physical contact as well. There were shoulders to graze with fingertips as they took seats at the table. There were hands to be touched while helping to chop coconuts. There were glutei maximi to be 'accidentally' bumped into when rummaging around in the supply hut. There were thank-you kisses from each woman—Mary Lynn's brief and chaste, Gina's lingering and wanton—whenever he did something helpful.

Accordingly, he found himself doing helpful things for them more and more as the days went by. Thus, the kisses kept coming. And his knowledge-base grew by leaps and bounds, particularly that which concerned the softness and sweetness of their lips.

Page after page of his journal became filled with both data and his interpretations of it. He had comparison tables galore, lists aplenty, and enough charts and drawings to send a rocket to Mars. He filled pages with speculations and musings and even went so far as to guestimate the cumulative degrees of arc that their many sets of curves might possess, from the undersides of their breasts, to their calves, to their almost spellbinding hips and behinds.

In only a few days' time, he determined that Gina's lips were plumper; Mary Lynn's were sweeter. Gina's skin was more electrifying; Mary Lynn's was more mesmerizing. Gina's touch was more evocative; Mary Lynn's, more suggestive. Gina's hair was softer; Mary Lynn's, prettier. Gina's smile was hotter; Mary Lynn's, warmer.

He took careful note of the ways in which various types of fabrics would lay across their breasts, whether that be loose and billowy, or tight and tempting.

He analyzed the soft and sultry waves of Gina's long, red hair as well as the cute and bouncy characteristics of Mary Lynn's pigtails.

He added paragraphs of observations on the unknowingly seductive swirl of Mary Lynn's tongue as she licked papaya juice off her lips, and the rather obscene way in which Gina slid bananas into her mouth.

He observed just how titillating Gina's wantonness could be, and how titillating Mary Lynn's lack of wantonness could be. After all, Gina worked hard to lure men in and she succeeded. Mary Lynn didn't seem to work at it at all and she succeeded every bit as well.

This last observation he found most fascinating of all.

On one particularly warm afternoon, he was rewarded with his best side-by-side view of the women thus far. He'd headed to the lagoon to check on the lobster traps, and there they were, on the beach, lying on a blanket, legs open slightly, sunning themselves in their bikinis: Gina's in deep red and Mary Lynn's in bright yellow. Their skin glistened beneath a well-applied slathering of suntan lotion.

Good Heavens! It had been quite some time since he'd last seen them lying in such a position — right beside one another and in bikinis, no less. Mary Lynn blushed modestly as he walked past and everyone exchanged smiles. Then, as he stood waist deep in the water, fiddling unnecessarily with one of the traps, he proceeded to cop eyeful after eyeful of them, trying to determine exactly what their warm, oiled skin would feel like against his.

Then it got better — much better.

Barely a minute after he'd waded in, he observed both women reaching into the coconut cup full of suntan lotion. Then they stood, bent forward, and began rubbing it into the backs of their legs. Thankfully, they were facing away from him—thankful, first of all, because they couldn't see him precision-ogling their every move; and, second, because he now had a direct line of sight to all the action taking place on the rear half of their anatomies not forty feet away.

And what mouth-watering action it was.

He tracked the movements of their four hands as they slathered more and more lotion over the entire lengths of their legs, from their ankles up to the exposed crescents of their behinds. Then Gina even hiked her bikini bottoms higher, exposing a good fifty percent of her exquisitely fashioned cheeks. He gasped and gaped as her hands rubbed lotion over every last exposed inch—slowly, tantalizingly—her palms and fingers working the lotion deep, deep into her apparently supple flesh.

And although innocent Mary Lynn predictably left her bikini bottoms unhiked, she, too, was now in the process of bringing gobs of the glorious goo onto her gorgeous glutes as well—the movements of her hands and fingers every bit as slow, every bit as tantalizing—her flesh every bit as soft, every bit as yielding to her touch.

And then—Heavens to Betsy!—each woman began to apply lotion to each other! First, Gina massaged it into Mary Lynn's bare and beautiful back, then Mary Lynn returned the favor, that is, after Gina removed her top, obviously in the name of obtaining an unobstructed tan. It was the most amazing view of either woman he'd ever copped. That lotion…their fingers…their warm flesh…their allure…

He could only imagine the sensations that each of their hands must have felt throughout this entire jaw-dropping process.

Finally, both ladies lowered themselves, face down, onto their towels, rewarding him with continued eyefuls of their resplendent curves.

By now the Doc was harder than a monkey wrench. He was grateful that his male organ remained hidden beneath the surface of the water as it throbbed, strained, and thrust outward from inside his swim trunks. It was a good long while before it retreated and he was able to get out of the water without embarrassment.

As he walked past them on his way back to the clearing, he stole one final peak at their slippery flesh. Yes, judging from the continued pulsations of his male organ, it was clear that further research was, indeed, called for.

He hurried back to the privacy of his hut, opened his science journal and began scribbling yet more of his findings on the incredible anatomies of his two subjects. Thus far, there was no clear winner; both women were continuing to offer up equally gratifying eyefuls of feminine allure, albeit in distinctly different ways.

With Gina, he hypothesized, it was mostly a matter of all that she offered.

With Mary Lynn, it was more a matter of all that she kept secret.

Then he smiled wistfully. If only he were to have the opportunity to explore their anatomies with his hands rather than merely his eyes. And if only he were to have the opportunity to do so without the impediment of clothing. Certainly, this would help to broaden the scope of his data immeasurably.

But his smile quickly turned rueful as he reminded himself that there was virtually no chance of any such opportunity arising for him, in this lifetime or the next.

CHAPTER THREE

Among the island's many blessings was an abundance of tasty foods from both the sea and the jungle. And among the castaways' favorites was the *'ohelo* berry, a delightfully tart offering that often found its way into their meals, both main dish and dessert alike. They always seemed to be in short supply, especially with Finnegan eating them like candy every chance he got. And so, the next afternoon, amidst late summer heat and humidity, Mary Lynn and Gina set out into the jungle, baskets in hand, in order to replenish their dwindling inventory.

They chatted as they picked and today's topic, Gina's favorite, was, of course, sex.

"I think you're holding out on me," Gina said tauntingly as they stopped beside a bush full of the succulent pink and red fruit and began filling their baskets.

Mary Lynn blushed and shook her head. "Gina, I swear, I'm not. I've told you the absolute truth."

"So, you've *never* had sex with a man…*ever*," Gina said dubiously.

"No, for the hundredth time, I *haven't*!"

"Not even oral?"

"Gina, no!"

"Oh, come on! Not even hand-jobs?"

"Gina, please! No!"

"I guess that rules out anal, then."

"Oh, for the love of god!"

"So, you're saying that, at twenty-eight years old, you're still a virgin."

Mary Lynn's blush grew deeper as she nodded. Chatting with Gina could get so uncomfortable at times. "Yes, I swear. First of all, Homer's Corners, Kansas is not exactly a den of impropriety like—"

"Like Hollywood?" Gina finished for her with a teasing grin.

"Well, yes, like Hollywood. And second of all, as you may have noticed, I'm not *that* kind of girl."

Gina sighed with an air of worldliness. "Girls who say they're not 'that kind of a girl' usually are and just won't admit it. Either that, or they secretly want to be. I mean, who wouldn't?"

Mary Lynn shook her head and shrugged. "Maybe I'm different, then."

Gina laughed as they continued further along the path through the jungle. "And maybe you're not!" She took a few more steps. "Anyway, did any boy ever try?"

"Oh, Gina, this conversation is becoming far too —"

"Never mind that!" Gina interrupted. "Just answer the question. After all, it's looking more and more like we're going to be stuck on this island for a long time...maybe even for the rest of our lives. Don't you agree that we should be totally open and honest with one another?"

Mary Lynn sighed and nodded. "I suppose so."

"Besides, I've told you my steamy stories, haven't I?"

She gave a short laugh. "Practically non-stop since I've known you."

Gina smiled saucily. "Exactly! Hey, what can I say? I like sex. I love it, actually. It's very good for you. And you've certainly enjoyed my stories, haven't you?"

"Yes, I admit I have but..." She sighed in defeat. "Okay, fine, I do have one story I guess I could share, all right?"

Gina's smile widened. "Now we're getting somewhere! Let's hear it!"

Mary Lynn shrugged once again. "Okay, here goes: One time, back in the fall of '63, I was at a drive-in theater with a fella I'd known from college…Jimmy Johnson. We'd been in many of the same classes and, oh, he was such a cute boy!" She giggled at the memory. "Anyway, about halfway through the first picture, he turned me toward him by my chin and said, very nervously, 'Mary Lynn, can I kiss you?'"

Immediately, Gina set her baskets of berries on the ground, took Mary Lynn's baskets from her hands, and set them beside the others. Then, grinning mischievously, she led her by the hands over to an enormous moss covered hollow log by the waterfall.

"Here we are. Now, just sit right back and tell me all about it!"

"Oh, Gina, I'd be too embarrassed. I mean, what if one of the others hears us?"

"Honey, so what if they do? Besides, we're all alone out here. Come on, tell me!"

Mary Lynn sighed. "Okay, fine. So, after a minute, I said yes and, well, we started necking."

Gina squealed hysterically. "Necking? Honey, nowadays we say 'making out.'"

"Okay, we started 'making out,' then. Oh, Gina, it was wonderful! His lips were so soft and gentle. They felt like velvet."

"Mmm. And was his tongue soft and gentle, too?"

Mary Lynn nodded, blushing once again. "Mm-hm. I can't even say how long we kissed, but it must have been quite a while. I never even saw the rest of the movie. But it was wonderful — the kissing, I mean — and it made me feel really strange inside, you know? Good-strange. Our tongues just kept dancing with each other and sliding across each other. And his hands were caressing the back of my neck and the bottoms of my ears the whole time."

Gina smiled and nodded as Mary Lynn's eyes strayed dreamily to the tops of the palm trees.

"Tell me more," Gina urged.

"Well, we were sitting in his '56 Ford pickup and I was slowly but surely sliding further forward on the seat. I was wearing one of my red gingham dresses and the hem was starting to creep up past my knees." She smiled again. "And it didn't take long for Jimmy to begin caressing my thighs. I was getting delirious at the feeling of his hand there, especially when it began to inch its way up and underneath the hem. I actually started to shiver and I think he did, too. Well, then he said, 'Mary Lynn, you have the most amazing legs, you know that? Every guy in college used to say the same thing.' Well, I just stared at him. I mean, I never knew that! 'They did?' I asked. 'What else did they say?' Jimmy blushed really hard, but he didn't answer. So, I asked him again, and he said...well, he said..."

49

Mary Lynn paused. This was starting to become a bit too awkward.

Gina looked up. "Oh, no, no, you're not stopping now! This is getting too good. Come on, tell me!"

Mary Lynn bit her lip, then sighed. "Well, he said the boys all agreed that I also had the nicest, um, butt on campus."

"Hm, no surprise there," Gina answered, matter-of-fact.

"Pardon?"

"Oh, come on, Mary Lynn! Do you mean to tell me you don't know? Honey, your ass is in a class by itself, okay? Seriously! *I'm* jealous of it. I mean, I know I have a great figure and all, but your butt is like *world*-class! It's incredible, actually."

Mary Lynn's mouth opened slightly. "Oh, my goodness. Seriously? You really think I have a nice behind?"

Gina shook her head. "Not just me, honey. I'm sure every man on earth would kill to get his hands on it. And, no, we're not just talking 'nice.' We're talking *astounding* here."

Mary Lynn's mouth opened wider. "Oh, my, I...I don't know what to say."

Gina laughed. "I know what you can say. You can say what happened next with Jimmy Johnson!"

Mary Lynn sighed wistfully. "There's not much more to tell, sadly. His hand went way up under my dress and I gasped a little. Well, maybe more than a little. His hand was all shaky and shivery as it slid over the top of my thigh and, of course, that made *me* all shaky and shivery, too. Then he said, 'Don't be scared, I just want to touch your panties a little, that's all.' He was so sweet and I guess I really did want him to touch me some more, so I nodded. A few seconds later, I squealed when I felt his thumb rubbing really gently against my...you know...my private parts."

"Your *pussy*," Gina corrected.

"Oh, Gina, please! Anyway, he was just grazing it a little, that's all. Still, it was enough to make me start getting a little delirious—"

"You mean *wet*," Gina corrected again.

Mary Lynn laughed in spite of herself. "Okay, 'wet,' then!" A pause. "Well, whatever it was, it was heavenly."

She paused again and smiled sadly. "But then, not ten seconds later, the car door on Jimmy's side was yanked open and there was my brother, Gregory...with my father's shotgun! Jimmy's hand flew out from under my dress pretty fast and before I knew what was happening, Greg yanked him out of the truck, socked him in the jaw, and said that if he ever caught him with me again, he'd have himself a 'ball-sack full of buckshot.'" She sighed once again.

"So, that was that. I didn't speak to my brother for weeks. And, of course, Jimmy made sure he stayed as far away from me as he could from then on."

"And you didn't go with any other boys after that?" Gina asked, her voice mildly incredulous.

"Not really. Between the work on our farm, and finding my first real job as a secretary in Winfield, there just wasn't time. Then, not long after that, I entered a sweepstakes that the local grange put on and I won an all-expense-paid trip to Hawaii." She shrugged. "And, well, you know the rest."

Gina sat shaking her head sadly and looking at Mary Lynn pityingly. "I just could *never* imagine not ever having sex." Then she laughed ruefully. "Of course, who am *I* to judge? Here I am, stuck on this island for three years now without a man. Me! Gina LaPlante — Miss Hollywood sexpot herself — with no man for three long, godforsaken years!"

Mary Lynn was shocked to see Gina's expression actually growing desperate — and then tears welling up in her eyes.

Then Gina simply broke down.

"Oh, Mary Lynn! I've been so horny for so long here I just can't stand it! I want a man so badly! I *need* a man so badly. I need a man to hold me and caress me and kiss me passionately and make love to me all night long. I need to feel him on me and in me and around me!"

She paused, sniffling. Then, more softly: "And you know what makes it even worse? There actually *is* a man on this island whom I'd do anything to get with and it turns out he has absolutely *zero* interest in sex...or women, for that matter." She laughed ruefully again. "I swear, I think the man would rather study a beetle than my pussy."

Mary Lynn's mouth and eyes opened wide. "You mean...*Doc*?"

Gina sniffled again. "Yes, *our* Doc. I mean, come on, Mary Lynn, don't try to tell me you've never admired his face or that gorgeous body of his. I saw you eyeing him up and down when he went out running the other day...for who knows what reason *that* was. Admit it: He looked damn good, didn't he?"

She blushed. "Well, yes, I did...and he did. But—"

"No buts. Admit it: The Doc's a hunk. A little too brainy for my taste, perhaps. But still, I could just eat him. And let me tell you something else: It's a sad shame to have a man with a face like his and a bod like his and he doesn't even know what to do with it! It's pathetic, really." She paused as she dabbed her eyes. "I would give anything just to hook up with him once. Mmm...maybe out by the ocean on a warm moonlit night...letting him go crazy on me right there on the sand...the waves lapping at our feet…ooh, la-la!"

As Gina spoke, Mary Lynn closed her eyes and found herself imagining that same scene unfolding with great clarity and intricate detail…except that it was *her* with the Doc…in the sand…the waves lapping at their feet.

Then Gina paused and sighed dejectedly. "Like that's ever going to happen."

"Maybe not," Mary Lynn admitted. "But I think I know of two other men who would positively jump at the chance to —"

"Jump *me*?" Gina finished for her with a faint smile. "Hey, don't I know it. The Captain and Finnegan have been eyeing me up and down pretty much nonstop since the day we set sail."

Mary Lynn nodded. "So I've noticed."

"Mm-hm. It's gotten pretty extreme, too." Gina grinned. "In fact, I've been spotting them with hard-ons practically nonstop lately. And do you want to know something? The last few times I've been showering over here under the waterfall, I've even noticed them spying on me with the Captain's binoculars — probably trading them back and forth the whole time — just peeping away."

Mary Lynn gasped and brought her hands to her cheeks. "Gina, no! Our Captain and our Finnegan?"

Gina answered with a slow, solemn nod. "Mm-hm."

"Don't tell me you were...bare!"

Gina gave a short laugh. "I was bathing, silly."

Mary Lynn gasped again. "Even when you knew they were watching?" She shook her head. "I can't believe this! The Captain and Finnegan have seen you? *Without your clothes on*?"

Now Gina collapsed into a fit of giggling. "Mary Lynn, you are positively puritanical!"

Ignoring Gina's comment, Mary Lynn closed her eyes and shook her head. "Well, it's a darn good thing that I bathe in the privacy of our hut, that's all I can say."

Gina smiled again. "You don't know what you're missing, honey. I happen to greatly enjoy the feeling of being peeped at. It's a very gratifying feeling of power, actually. I mean, for those few minutes, I *own* them! They are under *my* power!" Then she sighed. "Of course, I'd like it a whole lot more if our disinterested Man of Science were to enjoy the view as well...ha, like that's ever going to happen."

As if on cue, both women stood, picked up their baskets, and began heading back to the clearing.

Along the way, Gina added, "You know, now that I think about it, maybe it's high time I gave our two randy sailors and their trusty binoculars a bit more for their money." She laughed gaily. "It'll be fun. And, hey, I might as well enjoy *some* titillation while I'm stuck here."

Mary Lynn glanced at her and shook her head in bemusement at Gina's unbridled wanton ways.

But after just a few more steps, she realized that all of Gina's talk about sex and loneliness and the Doc was beginning to steer her own thoughts to a place which, admittedly, they'd been to more than a few times before. What, for instance, would it be like to make out with the Doc for an hour? Even better than with Jimmy Johnson, no doubt. What would it feel like to have *him* slide his hand up underneath her gingham dress and touch her the same way Jimmy Johnson had—and this time without interference from her brother? What would it feel like to have him make love to her?

Yes, she'd been around this block before. But now, these same thoughts and images seemed to have intensified to a whole new and beguiling level.

She smiled inwardly. *Gina thinks she's the only one who wouldn't mind being seduced by the Doc. Well, I've got news for her. There's someone else on this island who, for once, wouldn't mind a bit of passion in her life, either!*

And, since she was, in fact, going on twenty-nine years old, she certainly had waited long enough!

* * * *

King Palawani and his advisor, Jia-banu, sat out upon the Grand Terrace overlooking the pristine Sea of Ever-Peace below while his young concubine, Midori, delicate as the wing of a butterfly, filled their bejeweled goblets with fermented papaya nectar and then slipped away.

Though diminutive, Jia-banu was a revered legend on the isle of Tiazanu. Indeed, the one-hundred-two-year-old sage was known throughout this region of islands and islets as a woman of limitless wisdom. She was so wise, many would say, that, through the use of her keen intellect alone, she had even achieved immortality. Although her face betrayed a woman who had lived long and learned much, her strong body, her never-ending perfect health, and her bright intuitive eyes were that of a woman no more than half her age.

The king had just finished explaining his utterly embarrassing male condition to Jia-banu and he now waited respectfully for several long minutes as she sipped the nectar and thought deeply on the matter.

Finally, she spoke, her voice soft and melodious.

"Nuna huana ho-hopu si balawa," she said, her lips curved into an almost imperceptible smile. *Our young king does, indeed, have his problems.*

"Bah! Young! I am now amidst my fifty-seventh journey around the Life-Star. I should hardly call that 'young.'"

Jia-banu offered him a scathing down-the-nose look. "Next to me, you are an infant."

Palawani bowed his head in deference.

Then, after another moment, Jia-banu continued. "Throughout my many years, I have heard numerous legends telling of fair-skinned and lovely young maidens from strange and distant lands who occasionally arrived upon these islands." She swept her arm from west to east, her movement encompassing the unending sea. "In one mysterious way or other, they would arrive. Maidens of unimaginable beauty, they were. Women of unfathomable physical allure, and hitherto unheard-of copulative capabilities and licentiousness. Maidens with hair the color of gold, of ruby, of henna. Maidens with breasts the size of ripe melons and hips rounder than round. Maidens of decadent cultures who spoke in strange tongues and who knew of the most remarkable and otherworldly ways to please a man…daring ways, naughty ways, ways otherwise unknown to all of us."

Palawani was listening with great interest, his tongue absently grazing his upper lip, his Royal Man-Lance beginning to dance.

Decadent? Daring? Naughty?

Jia-banu smiled once again. Somehow, she always appeared to know what he was thinking.

She gazed off absently. "I always wondered if any of these legends could possibly be true."

Then she turned to him and peered deep into his eyes. "Perhaps it would be well for you to search for an answer and, by the grace of the gods, seize one of these exotically beautiful maidens for yourself."

Palawani gasped softly, his mind conjuring up just such an image. "But how?" he asked, his voice nearly pleading.

Jia-banu laughed softly now. "The 'how' is the easy part." She took his hands in hers. "Here is what you are to do: You are to send out an expedition to search every island you can reach for the existence of such maidens. You will conscript the service of forty young, able-bodied men, divided into eight squads of five men and three kayaks each. Two men shall occupy the first kayak, two men, the second, and one man, the third. This will, of course, leave room for the maiden...*if* one is to be found. Then she will be brought back to you and your, shall we say, 'deprivation' will come to a climactic end."

Palawani drew his hand from hers and began scribbling her instructions as fast as he could upon a dried banana leaf.

"Each squad is to be armed with blowguns," Jia-banu went on. "They will carry darts of lethal curare poison, should the removal of any maiden be met with resistance from her people. They will also carry darts dipped in an aromatic oil prepared from the herb *artemisia annua,* which will render the maiden safely unconscious for a short time. The preparation of these darts will be an easy task for your medicine man and they will afford your men the opportunity to capture, bind, and place her into the kayak without struggle."

Palawani finished writing, then looked up, for Jia-banu had stopped speaking.

"Could it truly be this simple?" he asked, still in awe at the very idea — the very daring and arousing idea.

She shrugged. "Simple to carry out? Of course. As for success? That, my friend, remains to be seen."

King Palawani picked up his royal conch shell and blew twice.

His assistant appeared at once and bent forward, offering his ear. The king spoke briefly to him, his voice hushed and intense.

The assistant straightened. "I will summon the medicine man immediately, My King. Then I will gather our forty best men to act as scouts. They will put their kayaks to sea at the morrow's first light."

Palawani smiled as he and Jia-banu returned their gazes to the vast Sea of Ever-Peace. At once his thoughts returned to those of exotic fair-skinned

maidens with hips rounder than round.
  And his Royal Peninsula rose in turn.

CHAPTER FOUR

At the day's first light, forty young and able-bodied tribesmen assembled at the beach on the northern tip of Tiazanu, where twenty-four exquisitely-fashioned sea kayaks sat in waiting. All of them wore royal red headbands, all had the bird-like image of the God of Sacred-Fertility painted upon their bare chests, and all sported fresh, new grass skirts from which hung their knives and machetes.

Boys and girls from the nearby village were scrambling about the kayaks, equipping each with food, water, medicinal herbs, tools, blowguns, sleep darts, and death darts, taking great care to stow the latter without touching the poisonous tips, an error which would quickly result in an unwelcome visit from the God of No-Life. Finally, the children placed brightly painted lanterns — blessed by King Palawani himself in the hope that the expedition would be met with success — upon the high bows of the outriggers.

As the men solemnly boarded the craft, they looked up the hillside where the king stood, offering his wave of good hunting.

Within minutes, they were atop the waves.

* * * *

As soon as Gina's eyes opened the next morning, she decided to take full advantage of the steamy late summer weather they'd been having, stay true to her word, and give the Captain and Finnegan a show they would never forget. She lay quietly in her bunk until she heard them outside tending to chores. Then she slipped silently out of bed, being careful not to wake Mary Lynn, and slipped into one of her most fetching dresses: the tighty-whitey number she'd made from Finnegan's old duffel bag, with *S.S. Moray* emblazoned up the side.

Minutes later, she emerged from the hut carrying her towel and a bar of their homemade soap.

"Morning, Gina!" the two sailors offered in unison as they tended to the fire they'd just started.

"Why, good morning, you two," she crooned.

"Well, well, you're up bright and early," the Captain commented, his eyes giving her a brief but very blatant up-down.

Finnegan's eyes narrowed and followed suit.

She smiled sweetly and stretched her arms out high and wide in what she decided must be the most provocative morning stretch ever performed. Then, in her sexiest voice, she replied, "Oh, I couldn't sleep, what with this heat and everything. So, I thought I might go take a nice *long* shower to help me cool off before breakfast." She swung her ass extra wide as she moved past them, then turned, wagged a finger playfully, and added, "And no peeping, you two!"

She could practically feel their eyes boring holes in the back of her dress as she slinked away.

No peeping? Ha! They'd be there. She knew they would, especially after those gaping stares they'd just given her. Well, today they were in for one hell of a surprise!

* * * *

The Doc opened the door to his hut just in time to see Gina exit the clearing carrying soap and a towel…and Finnegan and the Captain watching her every swaying move while practically foaming at the mouth the whole time.

He might have simply chuckled at the sight. But then, still watching, he saw Finnegan dive into their hut, then race back outside five seconds later carrying the Captain's binoculars. The two of them snickered wickedly just before tiptoeing from the clearing upon the same path that Gina had just taken.

He smiled faintly and nodded.

He could certainly put two and two together.

Then he rubbed his chin thoughtfully. Of course, now that he thought about it, perhaps...

* * * *

Gina had no sooner arrived at the base of the tiny waterfall and begun to slip out of her dress when she heard the faintest rustling in the jungle behind her. She forced down a grin. Well! They'd certainly wasted no time following her today!

She smiled and took a deep breath. "I do believe it's time to start the show!" she murmured.

Humming sweetly, she continued to slide the dress over her head, then laid it upon a rock beside her. Next, still facing away from the spot she knew they were hiding in, she reached back and unhooked her bra, freeing her breasts from their confines. After laying it upon her dress, she hooked her thumbs into the waistband of her panties and, ever so enticingly slowly, began to pull them down. Around the generous curves of her hips, she pulled. Over the hills and dales of her oft-lauded tushy, she tugged. Down the lengths of her lengthy thighs, she drew.

Once they were off, she dropped the panties to the ground, seemingly by accident. Then, grinning wickedly, she bent way down to retrieve them, giving her two Peeping Toms a good lingering look at her splayed cheeks, feeling the misty spray of the water against them, and enjoying the many delicious tingles that followed.

"How's that, boys?" she whispered as she stepped beneath the edge of the water and, still humming, began to rub the soap over her body. "Did you enjoy that? Well, don't go anywhere. That was just the, um, opening."

Turning toward the spot where she could just make out the glint of sunlight reflecting off the lenses of the binoculars through the jungle growth, Gina began to move the soap across her prized breasts. Back and forth she rubbed, first the left, then the right. She'd known for years that her boobies were veritable show-stoppers, so she spent a good long while on each one, making sure that both men had their fill. Not an inch was left un-soaped — not the fronts, not the sides, not the undersides, not her puffy nipples. She could all but feel their eyes closely following the movements of her fingers as they moved across the slippery, sudsy surface of each one and — *mmm* — that thought felt just as delicious as the touch itself.

Then, after spiraling the soap downward to lather her yummy tummy, Gina spread her legs and began to rub the soap sensually over and between them. Round and round and up and down, first one, then the other, she rubbed. First her shins, then her calves. Next her knees, then her thighs. Higher and higher she went until the soap was just starting to graze her pussy. *Ooh!* Everything was slippery, everything was soaking wet, and everything felt *so* good, adding an extra little zing to the thrill of her exhibitionism.

Around and around her lonely pink lips she moved the soap — slowly, tauntingly, passionately — for her pleasure as well as theirs.

"*Ooh!*" she called out dramatically, the performer in her enjoying the show as much as her libido. "*Ooh...ahhh...*yes, that's *so* good!" She rubbed faster, then began to moan, gasp, and fling her head from side to side in order to better sell her ecstasy.

Then she turned around again and began rubbing the soap across every inch of her glistening ass, squeezing each cheek hard, sudsing each of them with utmost care, gliding the soap from one end of her crack to the other, and then thrusting the whole package toward her onlookers with impunity.

"*Ooooh! Mmmm!*"

And all the while, she daydreamed that it was, in fact, the Doc using that soap on her right now...everywhere on her — both for her pleasure as well as his own—getting her squeaky clean and wonderfully slippery inside and out as she remained bent over beneath the spray. She dreamed of him carrying her in his arms to the soft bed of moss beside the waterfall and laying her gently upon it. She pictured herself lying back, stretching her arms above her head, and spreading her long thighs from stem to stern, the miraculous sight causing her man to gasp every bit as loudly as she intended to gasp just as soon as he plunged his cock inside her.

* * * *

"Un-be-*lieve*-able!"

"Talk about a fucking soap opera!"

The Captain and Finnegan had their heads squashed together as they each peered through one eyepiece of the Captain's trusty Navy binoculars, watching in awe as Gina moved the soap over and around her slippery body beneath the waterfall.

"Can you believe this, Cap'n?" Finnegan hissed, rubbing his tortured member inside his white sailor pants. "Look! Look what she's doing with that soap!"

"I...I'm looking, little buddy, I'm looking!" the Captain panted, his mouth open wide. He, too, had his free hand down his pants, tugging at his other little buddy as he gaped in disbelief. "I've never seen anything like this in my entire life! Look, little buddy! Just look at our Gina go!"

"Oh, I'm looking, Cap!" Finnegan whispered between groans. "But y'wanna know something? It just ain't fair that she should have to do all that to herself when there are two able-bodied seamen who would gladly help her out with that soap!"

"You're absolutely right, Finnegan," the Captain replied, squinting his viewing eye tighter as Gina, once again, slid the bar of soap round and round her beautiful fiery bush. "It isn't fair and it isn't right."

"Sure looks good, though, doesn't it?" Finnegan enthused, licking his upper lip.

He watched some more.

Then Finnegan's jaw simply dropped wide open. "Wait a minute...is she—? Is that—? Oh, my god, Cap! Look what she's doing *now*!"

"That—that's impossible!"

"Oh, yeah? Look!"

"This is...this...it's...just..."

"What a woman!"

They looked.

They gasped.

And they moaned.

Gina had that soap right...up...

Suddenly, without much in the way of warning, both men exploded into orgasms right there in the lush undergrowth, both men whipping off their hats and biting into them in order to stifle their moans and grunts, both men rolling over and over on the ground and flouncing recklessly against one another, both men twisting and squirming like worms on a griddle.

Then, after several seconds of tandem panting:

"Man, what I wouldn't give to have helped her do that!"

"Same here, little buddy," the Captain replied between pants. "I would've done anything to help her clean up that act of hers. But on the other hand, at least *we* have the satisfaction of knowing that we're the only two men on earth lucky enough to have just witnessed Gina LaPlante's greatest performance ever!"

* * * *

Meanwhile, not thirty yards to the Captain's left…

"Oh, my word! What manner of…masturbation…?"

The Doc was lying stiffly on the ground, dividing his time between peering through his own binoculars at Gina's sudsy show-of-shows, squeezing his spasmodically throbbing appendage, making copious notes in his journal, and moaning.

Never in his life had he ever beheld or, indeed, been aware of, such an act. It stunned him to watch Gina's bar of soap slip-sliding around the outskirts of her sex and then deep inside her womanly orifice. It stunned him and fascinated him. To think that any woman would even think to pleasure herself like that!

Indeed, it stunned him, fascinated him, and aroused him mercilessly.

What a sight Gina made as she stood beneath the falls with her legs spread so impossibly wide. He gasped when, for the second time, she turned, bent over, and moved the bar of soap down her back, down to her waist, down and across her spanking clean posterior, down...down...at last returning to her no longer private recess.

Had this woman no code of decency whatsoever, he asked himself, deliriously thrilled for the moment that, apparently, she did not.

"*Yesss!*" he heard Gina hiss as she threw her head back, her long, wet, red hair now a tangled and tantalizing work of art across her back. "*Ooh, yes, yes, yessss!*"

The Doc's mouth hung wide open, forgotten.

Then, without much in the way of warning, Gina LaPlante began to come.

"Oh...oh...oh, my god!" she cried out, convulsing wildly as she plunged the soap again and again up inside her slickened and very clean folds. Then she dropped to all fours, shoulders to the ground, spread her legs once again, and continued with the soap as she bucked back and forth, clawing at the ground, and moving her head in all directions. *"Oh…my…god!"*

Suddenly, right in the midst of it all, the Doc dropped his binoculars, whipped open his trousers and began yanking at his male organ like he'd never done before.

Which, in fact, he never had.

In barely ten seconds, he was finished.

Then, as he lay panting, he picked up his pen once again and wrote a brief passage while simultaneously taking quick peeps at Gina as she began to dry off:

Good heavens! Our beautiful and shameless Gina has just unknowingly offered me a most outlandish performance. Using a bar of soap around and within her vaginal canal, she has just finished masturbating both herself and me into overwhelming tandem climaxes. Her movements, her vocalizations, her licentiousness, and, of course, her very well-shaped body have come together, as it were, to provide me with the greatest carnal thrill I've ever experienced. No doubt, Gina scores very highly in all areas of physical form and prowess of sexual titillation.

Further study is, of course, warranted and I am most assuredly up for the endeavor.

* * * *

After Gina finished drying off and began to put her clothes back on, she noticed that the glint from the Captain's binoculars was no longer there. In fact, there was no sign of either Peeping Tom whatsoever.

Oh, well, she surmised, maybe they'd just gone off to be alone with their dirty thoughts.

But just then, a sharp glint of reflected sunlight emanating from the jungle to her right caught her attention. Without turning her head fully in that direction, she scanned the area and was surprised to see gleaming evidence of binoculars coming now from this new vantage point.

That's strange, she thought. Why would Finnegan and the Captain have moved over there? And how did they manage to do it so quietly? She had no answer to either question — until, while casually glancing in the same direction a moment later, she caught a glimpse of...no, not the Captain...and not Finnegan. No, it was — she peered harder — it was...

Gina gasped. It was the Doc! His white shirt was just peeking through the undergrowth. And then, for just a second, the top of his head popped into view, then retreated from sight.

"Well, well, well," she whispered, smiling her widest smile of the morning. "What do you know? The man has a dick after all. My, my, my."

Then, without much in the way of warning, Gina found herself getting wet all over again.

She pursed her luscious lips. Now that she thought about it, she'd have sworn she spotted the Doc eyeing Mary Lynn's ass last night at dinner, when she'd bent down for some reason or other. Twice, in fact.

And here she was, thinking it was nothing but a coincidence.

Well, apparently not!

So, Mr. Man of Science liked girls, did he? Well, well, well.

Gina finished putting on her dress, then picked up her towel and began walking slowly back to her hut. Along the way, she wondered how much peeking the Doc had done at *her* ass — that is, before today. After all, it certainly wouldn't be fair for him to be squandering too many of his newfound hard-ons on Mary Lynn, what with the innocent little farmgirl having virtually no experience in matters of making men hot and horny. Well, she did! Years of experience. On screen and off. Hollywood, Broadway, and everywhere in between. Actors, producers, and directors galore. She had heaps of experience behind her. Behind her, on top of her, and beneath her as well. Besides, *she* was the movie star here. And furthermore, she herself was the one who wanted the Doc so badly she couldn't stand it. It was high time he started checking out her world-renowned goodies for a change.

As, apparently, he just had.

And which she would make damned sure he did again, maybe even with his hands next time.

Then, with any luck, he and she would make sweet and sassy love happily ever after.

* * * *

For the rest of the day, Gina stayed on top of Doc at every turn. Though she tried her best not to arouse anyone's suspicion, she nonetheless took every opportunity to make sure that he noticed her. If she could give him an eyeful or two of her cleavage, she'd do it. If she could maneuver her ass into his line of sight here and there, she'd do it. If she could subtly raise a hem anytime he walked by, she would do that, too—and hopefully give him a rise in the process.

Likewise, if there was an opportunity to try and squeeze through the door to the supply hut just as he was coming out, she seized it and seized it good. If there was an opportunity to 'accidentally' leave the door to her hut open just before he walked by, just as she was in the middle of 'changing' her dress, she took it. If there was a moment during mealtime when she could regale everyone, including him, with yet another story from her Hollywood days that involved her in any one of the sixty-nine positions, she grabbed it.

Taken individually, neither of her actions would likely be regarded as greatly arousing to anyone, including the Doc. But cumulatively, she was quite certain they were doing their job of keeping his eyes and thoughts on her and her alone.

Now, if only his hands would follow suit.

And she had that plan figured out in about two minutes' flat.

CHAPTER FIVE

As had been his routine of late, just as the sun was making its first appearance over the lagoon, the Doc awoke, good and hard, following a very lucid dream in which Gina and Mary Lynn had their beautiful lips and hungry hands all over him at the same time, as he lay nude upon the beach. It was quite detailed and very realistic, in a surreal sort of way. He was just about to get out of bed to write about it when he heard a quiet tapping on his door. As he threw on his standard-issue white button-down shirt and khaki trousers, he could see through the bamboo door that it was Gina waiting outside.

Of all people.

She looked worried — fetching as well, in her form-fitting cream satin dress, but worried nonetheless.

He opened the door. "Gina," he said, his voice filled with concern. "Come in. What's wrong?"

Slowly, she came inside, closed the door behind her, and turned to him.

"Doc, I have to talk to you," she said, her tone very serious, indeed.

"Of course, dear. Whatever's the matter?"

She smiled sheepishly and lowered her eyes. "Well, it's a little embarrassing…"

He nodded and waited for her to continue.

"I think I may have found a lump."

He stared blankly. "A lump?"

"On my…breast." Then, with suddenly tear-filled eyes: "Oh, Doc, I'm so scared! What if—? What if it's—?"

The Doc swallowed hard and felt himself growing hard at the same time. After three years on this island together, this was the first time that anyone had come to him with a medical problem that could be described as serious, let alone 'intimate.'

He was certainly no medical doctor. And yet, who else could she possibly turn to in this matter?

It was up to him to—he swallowed again—lend her a hand.

"Now, now, Gina, calm down. It's probably nothing serious."

"But, Doc, what if it *is* serious?" Her voice was growing more panicked by the second.

Oh, dear. He needed to help the poor girl.

And, of course, that meant…

Yes, someone was going to have to examine her. And that someone, of course, needed to be him.

Suddenly he was stiff as a tire iron and jittery as a misaligned front wheel.

He was going to have to examine Gina LaPlante's breast.

With his hands.

His science journal was soon to receive its most informative entry yet.

His research was about to rise to a whole new degree of credibility.

He barely looked her in the eye as he said, "Gina, please, calm down. Why don't we take a, um, look and see if there really is cause for concern?"

Gina's look of panic disappeared immediately. "Oh, Doc, that would be wonderful! Would you? I...I mean, I know I'll be so very embarrassed, of course. After all, I've never, you know, shown my breasts to you before. But, well, this *is* for an important reason, after all."

"Why, yes, it most certainly is," he replied, his voice remaining somber just as he felt a certain small dripping down his leg. "Now, in order to proceed, I'm afraid you're going to need to lower the top of your dress and remove your, um, your..."

"My bra?"

"Yes, um, that. You'll...need to remove... your...your...um, yes..."

Gina lowered her eyes. "I understand, Doc. Whatever you say." Without waiting for a reply, this beautiful, well-endowed movie star reached up and pulled the straps of her dress off her shoulders, allowing it to fall. It slipped down her torso, coming to rest upon her wide hips, exposing her pink bra and the lacy waistband of her matching panties. She looked down at her cleavage for a moment, then back up at him, swallowing hard while at the same time offering a slow, trusting blink.

It was all the Doc could do to keep from fainting dead away as he took in the sight of Gina undressing not two feet in front of him. He simply could not believe what was about to happen. He just hoped that he wouldn't spill his seed right in front of her. That would, of course, be most awkward — for both of them.

Then, very slowly, Gina slipped the bra straps from her shoulders, first one...then the other. The poor girl! She must be finding it quite difficult to expose herself in front of him like this.

Nonetheless, after taking a deep breath, she did manage to reach back and unhook it.

Then, holding the cups against herself, she took another deep breath, swallowed very hard one last time, closed her eyes, and...

At that exact moment, the door opened and Finnegan burst inside.

"Hey, Doc, have you seen Gi —?"

His jaw dropped. His eyes bugged out of his head.

And there was Gina, having just taken off her bra, standing right there in front of both men with her shapely, nude breasts welcoming his arrival.

Just then, her dress slipped off her hips and dropped to the floor, exposing both her snug pink panties and her long, curvilinear thighs.

Finnegan's eyes shot downward to behold both the miracle of gravity and the wonder of symmetry. "N-never mind," he said, his mouth opening and closing repeatedly. "I guess you already have."

"Finnegan!" the Doc and Gina yelped in unison.

Gina quickly covered herself with her hands.

"We are conducting a very serious medical examination here!" he shouted. "Leave at once!"

Finnegan didn't seem to know what to do. He politely removed his hat and nodded to Gina, he turned his head from side to side, and his mouth continued to open and close. "I...I...I'm sorry. I'll just...I'll just let myself out. Um, see ya." His eyes never left Gina's body as he started backing up toward the door.

Finally, he whirled and dove back outside.

A second later, the Doc turned back to Gina as she stood before him in nothing but her panties. His own eyes opened wide and he very nearly died as a result of the miraculous and overpowering sight before him. Gina's handheld breasts, her hips, her legs — they were works of art, every one. He could have beheld them all day.

Alas, he had work to do.

He released a shaky sigh. "I'm very sorry about that, Gina."

"Oh, it's all right, Doc," she replied, lowering her hands to her sides once again — revealing herself to him once again.

Another sigh. "Very well, let us proceed then. Which, um, breast has the suspected lump?"

"This one." She pointed to her left breast.

"Very well. I believe the correct procedure is for you to —" He cleared his throat. "To place your left hand behind your head."

"Oh, um, okay. Well, here goes." Slowly, she did exactly as he'd instructed.

Naturally, this caused her breast to thrust toward him just a tad further.

He gulped.

He took a step toward her.

Then, slow as a sea turtle on life-support, he reached out and placed his two hands upon it.

Ah, skinfall.

It was the most wondrous thing he'd ever experienced in his life. Softer than soft. Smoother than smooth. Gina's breast filled his hands exquisitely as he cupped it from below, then used the fingertips of his free hand to begin pressing into her downy flesh in small circles — feeling... exploring...savoring...and, of course, researching.

At one point, he looked up at Gina briefly. She was staring up at the roof of the hut, biting her lip, and taking deep breaths.

And, unless he was mistaken, he could have sworn he heard her moan.

Then, seconds later, he heard it again. Yes, it was most assuredly a moan — a long, barely audible moan.

Oh, the poor girl! She must be terribly embarrassed. What an ordeal for her to have to go through.

But press on, he must.

And so, he continued, pressing now a bit deeper, a bit more audaciously into her, first on the sides, then underneath, then straight on. But, no matter where he felt, he couldn't locate a single lump anywhere. He pressed deeper still. Nothing. He squeezed from all sides, practically fondling the amazing, silky breast of this stunning world-famous actress. Nothing.

Meanwhile, his male organ continued to throb. More dripping down his leg occurred, especially when he took her plump pink nipple between his fingers and squeezed it. Just to be sure.

Gina gasped.

Startled, he released it immediately.

Well, after all, isn't that what doctors did? He'd have sworn he heard about it once from a university colleague who specialized in women's medicine.

But in the end, there was no lump to be found. Reluctantly, he removed his hands and shook his head.

"I'm sorry, Gina, but I can't seem to find..."

Gina looked panicked. "Oh, please, please, keep trying, Doc. It's *got* to be there somewhere. It's just got to." Then: "Oh, um, on the other hand, maybe it's the right breast, now that I think about it. I was so upset, I might have been mistaken." She tilted her head disarmingly and pointed toward the other breast. "Do you think you could try that one...just to be sure?"

Gallantly, the Doc took her right breast in hand and continued his examination. Gina needed him after all; he wasn't giving up.

He persevered. He pressed on. He squeezed on.

Gina moaned once again.

And his male organ throbbed accordingly.

"Well, Doc?" she asked softly a few moments later, her voice breaking his runaway train of thought.

"I...I'm sorry, Gina, I just can't seem to find..."

He felt her just a bit longer.

And then, seconds later, he did, in fact, feel a bit of hardness between his thumb and index finger. It wasn't a lump, though; obviously just a bit of natural ligament. He wondered if this was what she'd found.

He felt some more—just to be on the safe side.

"Mm-hm," he uttered in a doctorly manner. "Mm-hmmm."

Finally, he sighed and then released her wondrous breast from his sweating hands.

He was surprised that Gina made no move to cover herself. She simply stood there, apparently awaiting his diagnosis.

"Well, Gina, I'm very happy to report that there is no lump whatsoever."

He smiled, modeling a feeling of relief for her.

Gina smiled in return. "Oh, um, that's wonderful news, Doc! Phew! I'm so relieved. And I'm sorry to have bothered you so early in the morning like this. I was just beside myself with worry, as you could only imagine." She shook her head and smiled depreciatingly. "Silly me."

"An honest mistake, Gina. The hardness you felt was simply ligament tissue, commonly referred to as 'Cooper's ligaments,' as I recall. They provide the breast with structural support...of which you appear to be in...abundant supply." He smiled at her once again. "Yes, your breasts are, um, quite healthy...quite healthy, indeed."

"You're the Doc," she said with a warm smile.

Curiously, she continued to stand before him in nothing but her sandals and panties.

"Well, I confess that I'm not an M.D. However, given what I do know about biology, along with the findings from my examination, I do feel qualified to assure you that your breasts are, again, very healthy. You have nothing whatsoever to worry about."

She smiled again. "Oh, Doc, you can't imagine how happy I am to hear that! I was so —"

Just then, the door to the hut opened once again.

"Hey, Doc, aren't you coming to —?"

And there was The Captain now filling the doorway. He took one look at Gina and performed the world's greatest double-take of all time.

His Captain's hat fell to the floor.

Again, Gina quickly covered herself with her hands.

"Oh, I'm sorry for barging in. I...I'm just...I mean, I didn't realize..."

"It's okay, Cap'n," Gina said reassuringly. "I thought there was a lump in my breast and Doc was just making sure I'm okay."

"Which, I am happy to report, she is," the Doc replied, smiling smugly and feeling rather superior at that moment.

The Captain retrieved his hat, then began backing up toward the door, his face beet red, his eyes now glued to Gina's crotch, and his own crotch swollen with gratitude. "Well, I'm glad to hear you're all right, Gina. I...I'm sorry for barging in. I guess I'll just go, um, help Mary Lynn set the table." He laughed nervously and nearly tripped over himself as he turned and hurried out the door.

The Doc turned back to Gina and the two shared a sigh of relief. Then Gina began to put her clothes back on.

And the Doc said good-bye to her unparalleled, unclothed female anatomy.

When she was dressed, she turned to leave.

The Doc lowered his hand to his crotch to cover the small wet spot on his trousers.

She stopped in front of the door and turned back.

"Thank you, again, Doc. It was very kind of you to help me." She leaned forward and gave him a soft, lingering kiss. A very lingering kiss, in fact.

No doubt merely a token of her gratitude.

He kept his hand safely in front of his crotch the whole time.

"Well, I guess we should go eat before Finnegan gets it all," Gina said, smiling sheepishly.

She opened the door, then stopped again. "Aren't you coming?"

"Um, yes, in a few minutes," he answered, wishing that his wild heartbeat would begin to decelerate from its breakneck tempo. "I just have a bit of, um, straightening up to do first."

Gina smiled — a rather curious smile — then turned and left. Immediately, the Doc changed into clean shorts and trousers. Then he went over to his writing table on wobbly legs, sat down, and opened his journal...

I have just experienced an experience to end all experiences. I have just given Gina's breasts a thorough tactile examination and it has left me dazed. Never in my life have I ever felt anything so incredible. Never have I even so much as imagined anything like this. Her flesh! So impossibly soft and alluring. It is indeed a veritable miracle of nature. I am dazzled to the nth degree and I now find myself as aroused as a bonobo monkey.

On a side note: I shall never forgive myself for having chosen the wrong doctoral degree in life!

Unfortunately, this experience now leaves my research skewed, for while I have now had the opportunity to behold Gina's natural unclothed beauty visually and to feel it within my hands as well, I've had no such opportunity with Mary Lynn. And, given her far greater degree of modesty, it is unlikely that one will ever be afforded me. This, I'm afraid, will leave my study with no firm or equitable conclusion whatsoever.

And so, for the first time in my life, I am at a loss as to how to proceed.

* * * *

A short while later, the Captain and Finnegan were down at the lagoon, untangling one of the fishing nets, comparing notes, and fuming.

"That lucky bastard," the Captain growled. "I don't see why he should be allowed to see Gina's boobs like that and feel them and — "

Finnegan moaned. "Holy shit! You mean he *felt* 'em, too?"

The Captain sighed and shook his head as he worked his half of the net. "Of course, he felt them, you numbskull! He must have! That's how you examine boobs, for goodness' sake."

"Why, that lucky, stinkin' son of a bitch," Finnegan echoed, as his half of the net became even more tangled. "Well, anyway, you're right, it's just not fair, Cap," he went on. "We like Gina just as much as he does. We do stuff for her, too. And I say that entitles *us* to feel her tits, too!"

The Captain sighed. "I'm with you, little buddy. But, face it, the Doc's more qualified to do that than we are. He knows about biology and things like that. Besides, he probably didn't even enjoy it. I'll betcha he probably just noticed her boob's medical condition or something like that, you know, the way a doctor would...instead of getting off on how ever-loving incredible it must've felt, the way a normal fella would. Gina probably figured she didn't have to worry about him trying to suck 'em or anything."

"Well, It's just not fair anyway!" Finnegan went on, two of his fingers now stuck in the knots. "Did you see those things? I mean, through the binoculars was one thing, but right there in front of our eyes...my god, they were fucking amazing! I could just kill myself for not being able to feel 'em up like he did."

"I know, little buddy, I saw them, too. And you're right: they *are* amazing. But there's no use either one of us getting all worked up about it because there's absolutely no way that we'll ever have the chance to do anything more than just look at 'em covered up, or see them through binoculars."

Finnegan was all but wrestling with the net by now, his hands and fingers becoming completely entangled in the process. "Well, that ain't fair either!" he replied, angrier than ever. "Some friend. The least he could have done was to invite us to stay and watch."

The Captain shook his head. "Little buddy, you are—"

"I know, I know," Finnegan cut in. "I'm one horny fella. Excuse me for having a dick."

* * * *

It was just after four a.m. when the Doc woke after yet another night of fitful sleep. Once again, images of Gina and Mary Lynn had barraged him mercilessly and he was now coming to the realization that, for all intents and purposes, they had been the totality of his thoughts and actions for over a week now. And for what good? Having already decided that his research project regarding their comparative beauty and sexual allure was now at a standstill, there really was no further point or purpose to his being distracted and sexually worked up throughout every waking minute.

Deeming any additional sleep to be out of the question right now, he sat up in his bunk, lit a candle, and, within a brief moment, came to a decision.

Bottom line: He needed some space, he needed to clear his head, and he needed to throw himself wholeheartedly back into doing the work that he was put on this island by the forces of fate to do. That work was the study of tropical flora and fauna—more specifically for right now: the mating rituals of the Mynah bird. He had been tracking the activity of a particular male and female Mynah for nearly a week, right before getting sidetracked by his own carnal urges, and it was high time he returned to it.

And so, while the rest of his fellow castaways slept in their nearby huts, and amidst the enchanting sounds of the tree frogs and other nocturnal creatures of the surrounding jungle, he dressed and then packed his knapsack with food, water, his binoculars, his journal, and pen.

Next, he wrote a note explaining that he would be on the far side of the island doing research for the entire day, then tacked it to the outside of his door. Finally, flashlight in hand, he headed into the dark jungle, happy to be leaving his preoccupations behind.

And curiously unhappy for the very same reason.

CHAPTER SIX

The sun was high overhead when the three sea kayaks made landfall upon this, the fourth island to be searched for maidens. Jianu, young tribesman and leader of the band assigned to sea-region five, scanned his surroundings intently as his boatman drew the craft up onto the small beach. Then he disembarked and waited for the others to gather round.

"Mi-nami kikala tiki-azu," he announced decisively. *We will find a maiden here.*

"How do you know this?" one of the men asked.

He pointed to several mysterious sets of footprints a bit further up on the beach and beckoned the others to follow him. "This is how I know." He knelt down and studied a few of the footprints carefully. "Look...such a strange shape. These must have been made by most unusual moccasins. People of far-off and exotic lands inhabit this island. I am sure of it. It is probable that there is a beautiful and suitable maiden among them."

He stood, then nodded toward the sea kayaks. "Hide these well, gather up our weapons, then come with me."

Soon, the men reached the crest of the hill and found that it overlooked much of the island. They stopped and began scanning the land that was spread out before them.

Seconds later, Jianu grabbed the shoulder of one of the other men and pointed toward a small beach on the edge of a lagoon.

"Look! It is as I said."

The men looked down and gasped in awe.

There, lying on the sand, perhaps one hundred-fifty paces away, were two women — two exotically hued women, lying upon the sand, each wearing two tiny pieces of fabric, one in yellow, the other in red. The fabric covered so little, that, even from this distance, it was plain to see that these women were, indeed, exquisitely formed.

As for beautiful? They were at too great a distance to tell, but Jianu could only assume that these women most certainly were. They had to be!

He nodded slowly. *King Palawani will be most pleased.*

"We must capture them," one of the men whispered.

"Not yet," Jianu replied. "They cannot be alone on this isle." He scanned more of the island, then pointed again. There, in a clearing not far from the lagoon, they could make out the figures of three men and a woman in the midst of several huts.

He nodded toward two of the men. "Make them sleep, then bind them. When you are finished, head toward the lagoon quickly. Together, we will capture the maidens."

"Why do we not kill them?" one asked.

Jianu shook his head. "They have not seen our arrival. They pose no danger to us. Now go."

The two men nodded and left.

Jianu turned towards the remaining tribesman. "Let us move closer while we wait. When the others return, we will capture them and choose the one who is certain to please Our King the most."

* * * *

The Captain never knew what hit him. One minute, he and Finnegan were doing patchwork on the supply hut, chatting with the Powells as they lay upon their lounge chairs. The next minute, he felt a tiny sting in the back of his neck and then…nothing.

* * * *

Neither Jianu nor his partner, Karuka, could take their eyes from the women. They had moved down the hill and through the jungle and were now crouched behind a bush at the edge of the small beach, barely ten paces from the—yes!—very beautiful maidens who appeared to be asleep as they lay upon colorful sheets of cloth. The two men peered intently at them, taking note of their soft, full curves, intriguing hair, and smooth, light skin.

Jianu smiled. Palawani would be most pleased, indeed.

"They are so beautiful," Karuka whispered, his voice barely audible. "Both of them. It is unfortunate that we cannot enjoy them for ourselves before returning one to Our King."

Jianu glared at Karuka fiercely. "And if we are found out, that would surely mean a visit from the God of Death-Lava for all of us, you fool!"

Karuka grinned. "Not to worry. I have an idea. After we choose which maiden to present to Our King, we will make her sleep and enjoy the other one right here for ourselves! Palawani will never know."

A smile spread slowly across Jianu's face and his being was at once filled with desire. Such an act would be most gratifying—particularly with one of these lovelies. Slowly, he nodded. "I believe your idea is a sound one. Just do not forget who is the leader—and who is first!"

Karuka grinned and began rubbing his man-part through his skirt. "Agreed. After all, in this case, I will have to wait for only a very short time!"

Suddenly Jianu whipped his knife from his belt and brought it dangerously close to Karuka's throat. "Perhaps you should put your energy to better use while we wait," he warned. "I will stay here and keep watch over our maidens. You, go collect many vines and place them behind those two posts over there where we will tie them up. Remain hidden at all times."

"Yes, Jianu," Karuka replied. Then, as he crept away: "I thank the God of Man-Joy for this day!"

* * * *

The three other tribesmen made short work of securely binding the arms and legs of their four sleeping captives, then dragged them over to the edge of the clearing and bound each of them with vines, in a seated position, to one of four adjacent trees. They completed their task by searching through the huts for pieces of cloth which they cut into strips and tied around their victims' mouths— should any of them awaken before the mission was completed.

After this was done, they hurried back toward the lagoon, anxious to begin the much more enjoyable work of capturing maidens.

* * * *

The Doc was in his glory as he moved quietly and attentively through the hot jungle, tracking the unmistakable calls of the two Mynah birds he believed were the same ones he'd identified the week before. He'd been tracking them for the past hour now and was convinced that they were preparing to mate.

And, armed with binoculars and his journal, he would be ready for them!

He made his way toward the west beach, listening intently. The two birds were on the move and not often in sight. However, by triangulating his position relative to the two distinct calls and then approximating the varying decibel levels between each of them and himself, it was a very simple matter to determine their relative location and distance.

He smiled. This was to be his greatest opportunity yet to observe and take richly detailed notes on their mating rituals! He couldn't wait to render the notes into a fascinating article for the scientific community, or, if they were never to be rescued, then at least for his own reading enjoyment in the years to come.

At the same time, he was relieved to be free, at least for the moment, from the stranglehold his thoughts surrounding Gina and Mary Lynn had had upon him. The fresh air out here by the ocean was a breath of fresh air in more ways than one.

Arriving at the edge of the beach, he directed his gaze to the trees off to the left—listening... scanning...

And there they were!

He quickly crouched down on the sand, grabbed his binoculars, and trained them upon his two beautiful and colorful subjects as they perched side by side upon an open branch with nothing but blue sky behind them. They were remarkable specimens as well, their feathers displaying nearly every color under the sun.

He waited, peering intently into the eyepiece, only briefly distracted by memories of the last time he'd used his binoculars. Gina's shower had been a mating ritual of a whole other order—one which he cared not to be burdened by at this time.

Right now, it was all about the beautiful creatures filling his viewfinder.

Just then the male inched closer. The female backed away.

He tried again. Once more, the female backed away.

He tried a third time—and this time the female remained where she was!

Then, together, the two birds swooped down to the ground and the male began to prance around in front of the object of his affection.

The Doc grinned widely. Yes! It was time. This was it!

But then, suddenly, he froze, for there, on the edge of the jungle, just to the left of the Mynahs, were three primitive sea kayaks.

He looked around to see if anyone was nearby.

Seeing no one, he ran over to them. Arriving at the nearest one, he reached out and ran his fingers across the beautifully carved inscription on the bow in an effort to determine which tribe of natives had arrived here.

He wracked his brain for a few seconds, then had his answer. Yes, of course! The natives of the island of Tiazanu were known for constructing kayaks with this type of detailing. And, thankfully, they were known for being a relatively peaceful people as well.

In fact, this could well be an opportunity for the rescue they'd all been waiting for. That is, if Tiazanu was anywhere near enough to the shipping lanes.

Without a second's hesitation, he threw his binoculars and journal into his knapsack, slung it onto his back, and began heading swiftly back to the clearing.

His amorous Mynahs would simply have to wait.

* * * *

Mmm…the early afternoon sunshine felt wonderful as usual, Mary Lynn noticed as she began to awaken from her nap. Yes, it was a magnificent day — magnificent and so peaceful.

Then, as she grew more alert, a troubling question arose in her mind:

Was it, in fact, *too* peaceful?

She lifted her head and turned it from side to side, listening intently.

It was the strangest thing. Normally, she would hear the nearly continual sounds of conversation and various daily activities emanating from the hut area less than a hundred yards behind her. But, as for this moment, all was still.

Uncomfortably still.

She raised herself up onto her elbows and listened some more.

Still nothing.

"Gina?" she said softly, her voice filled with unease. "Gina? Please wake up."

Gina's eyes fluttered open. "Hm? What is it, Mary Lynn?"

She shook her head. "I don't know. Something doesn't seem right. It's too quiet."

Gina sat up and listened for a moment. "I don't hear anything."

Mary Lynn sat up beside her and shook her head again. "That's what I mean. I don't hear anything, either. But that's what bothers me. Back in Kansas, the farmers have a saying: Never trust the wolves that you *can't* see."

Gina laughed softly. "There you go again with your farmgirl superstitions." She stretched her arms luxuriously, then reached over for the coconut cup filled with the Doc's suntan lotion and began rubbing some more onto her legs. "Listen, with Finnegan usually causing some form of ruckus or another, I happen to enjoy a rare moment of quiet like this."

"Well, I do, too...if only this quiet weren't *quite* so...so —"

That was as far as she got.

Suddenly, she and Gina gasped as powerful male hands swept around them from behind and clamped tightly over their mouths, stifling any screams that would have followed. She instinctively began to struggle and squirm, but only for an instant, for, before she could catch her breath, three natives leaped in front of them, all brandishing machetes.

She turned her head toward Gina, whose eyes were wide and frantic above the top of the man's hand that covered her mouth.

"No sound. No fight," one of the men with a machete warned. "You understand? Or else..." He drew his machete menacingly across his throat.

She nodded, scared out of her mind. Gina nodded as well.

"Stand," another commanded.

They stood. Mary Lynn instinctively covered the front of her body with her arms and hands.

"Now...walk!"

Mary Lynn shook as she and Gina were brought to the opposite side of the beach where stood the two posts that the men used to hang the fishnets on. Then she felt herself being turned around and maneuvered back up against one of the posts. Out of the corner of one eye, she saw that Gina was suffering the same fate.

Then, faster than she would have thought possible, Mary Lynn felt her body, from her breasts to her ankles, being lashed tightly against the post with dozens of vines.

She looked into the eyes of one of their captors as the other men finished binding them. He was obviously the leader, for the others kept deferring to him and asking him questions as they worked. Thankfully, he didn't seem at all savage or even mean—merely determined.

And yet, here they were, tied to posts in nothing but their bikinis, exposed and vulnerable, in front of five young male natives.

Savage or not, this could not be good.

After the men were finished, the hands were taken from their mouths.

"No sound!" the leader repeated. "Others all captured. Not help you."

"What do you want from us?" she whispered pleadingly. She had a feeling she knew.

But the answer that came was not what she expected.

It was worse. Much worse.

"Our king, Palawani, want new maiden. Take one of you to him. It not bad thing. You live with kindly king in beautiful palace. Have many riches. One of you very lucky."

She and Gina gasped in unison.

"You're going to…to *take* one of us?"

"Which—?" Gina swallowed. "Which one?"

"Not know yet. Must choose," the leader replied. "Must decide who better. Little one…" He trailed his fingers through Mary Lynn's hair, down her cheek, then below her chin.

She gasped and forced her eyes shut.

Then he turned to Gina and ran his fingers from her chin down to the peaks of her breasts. "Or big one." Gina held steady, looking straight ahead, doing her best not to look afraid.

Then the leader stepped back and scanned both of them from head to toe, smiling an appreciative smile that made her skin crawl.

His four accomplices did the same, their heads moving almost in unison from one woman to the next—up then down, then back up again. Mary Lynn had never felt more humiliated in her life. She looked over at Gina and was almost surprised to see that, for once in her life, Gina was not enjoying all the male attention.

Next, the five natives launched into a heated argument. Mary Lynn looked from man to man, wishing at the very least that she could understand what was being said.

A moment later, the argument ceased and the leader stepped close to her and Gina once again. "Cannot decide which one to take to King Palawani. Men want to take both, but only room in kayak for one." A long uncomfortable pause. "Must choose. Somehow."

Once again, he stepped back and the five captors resumed their argument. Every so often one of them would point to her or Gina—to various parts of their bodies—and all she could do was stand there, practically naked, and shiver uncontrollably as they did.

Then it happened. The leader stepped between them again. "Hard to decide what King want more...tall woman with hair color of fire and long legs to wrap around him...or little one with face of angel and who look like *true* maiden."

Then an utterly awful smile came over his face. "Must see more."

Mary Lynn froze. "Oh, please...no," she whispered, shaking her head from side to side.

"Please...don't," she heard Gina plead.

Acting as if he hadn't heard, the leader's hand moved slowly toward her.

Mary Lynn shook her head harder and her breath was now nothing but a series of gasps.

Then she felt his fingers grasp the strap of her bikini top.

CHAPTER SEVEN

As the Doc neared the clearing, he was almost beside himself with excitement. Whatever the reason for the Tiazanu natives to be here, there was every possibility they could help them get back to civilization.

Whatever their reason, he was sure it was good news.

His entire perspective changed the instant he entered the clearing and saw Finnegan, the Captain, and the Powells unconscious and tied to four trees. He dropped his knapsack to the ground and knelt beside the Captain, noticing immediately the tiny dart in the back of his neck. He gently removed it, then removed the three darts from the others and held them under his nose. *Artemisia annua*, he determined. Perfectly harmless anesthetic.

He sighed. That, at least, was a relief.

He began to untie the Captain. But no sooner had he gotten his hands free, the Doc froze, his heart caught in his throat. He whipped his head from side to side, growing more panicked by the second.

Where were the women?

In barely a split-second, he had it all figured out. He scrambled to his feet, then raced off in a frantic search, first in their hut, then toward the lagoon.

Thankfully, he heard the voices of the natives just before he emerged from the jungle. Otherwise, he might have run right straight into the midst of the horrific scene that was unfolding before him.

His heart caught in his throat. There were Mary Lynn and Gina tied to the fishnet posts, surrounded by five young native tribesmen.

And one of them was reaching for the strap on Mary Lynn's bikini.

The Doc whirled and raced back to camp. He dove into the supply hut and reemerged not five seconds later carrying the flare gun and the last three flares they had — flares which they had been saving for times when it seemed likely that ships or planes might be in the area.

Flares which, in recent months, no one had seemed all that interested in using.

He flew back down to the lagoon, loading the gun as he ran, and arrived just as he heard Mary Lynn and Gina cry out.

"Please! No!"

He dove out from the jungle and onto the beach.

"*Stop!*"

The five natives whirled and, brandishing their machetes, started toward him.

They'd only made it about two paces when the Doc opened fire with the flare gun, shooting straight into a bush just a few feet to the left of where the natives stood. The noise alone was enough to stop them in their tracks. But then the flare exploded, sparks flew out, and the bush went up in flames. Now the superstitious natives stared in shock at the spectacle, inching backward away from him, away from Gina and Mary Lynn, and away from the flames.

He reloaded and fired again. Seconds later, a second bush ignited, this one even closer to them.

The tribesmen leaped back in utter horror.

"Behold! I am the Great God of Death-Fire!" the Doc shouted in his deepest and most commanding voice. "Be gone! Be gone before you are all struck by a horrible burning death!"

The natives' look of shock and fear multiplied. Their eyes opened wide and two of their machetes fell to the ground.

"Mahula-humba! Mahula-humba!" they all shouted at once.

Then, without taking one more look at the women, the band of tribesmen leaped onto the path that headed toward the beach where they'd stowed their kayaks and raced off, still screaming in panic and dread.

The Doc raced off after them. "I'll be right back, girls!" he called over his shoulder. "Don't worry!"

Between all the commotion and the fact that he'd placed all his attention on the tribesmen, he didn't yet realize that both women were now topless.

He sprinted through the jungle, pulling the last of the flares from his pocket and loading it into the gun as he ran.

One flare left. He prayed it would be enough.

Two minutes later, he ran out onto the beach, gasping for breath, just as the natives were frantically pulling their kayaks into the water, still babbling hysterically.

"Go! Leave the Isle of Death-Fire and never return!" he shouted. "Go! Go!"

Then, just as they were pushing off, he took careful aim and fired his last round. It hit the sand not two feet from them. Sparks exploded out, some leaping onto their bare backs as they fought to get their boats out and moving.

Their screams were all the reassurance the Doc needed. That had to hurt. They would not be back. Nonetheless, he waited until they were well out to sea, rowing insanely, before he turned and ran back to the lagoon.

A veil of smoke from the two burning bushes met him as he ran out onto the beach, obscuring his view of Gina and Mary Lynn, who were now coughing uncontrollably. He snatched up a bait bucket and used it to scoop water out of the lagoon to throw onto the burning bushes. It took more than a dozen dousings before the fires were safely out and he was able to turn his attention to the women.

Then he gasped.

There were Mary Lynn and Gina, standing tied to the twin posts, still coughing, and wearing nothing but their bikini bottoms.

In all the excitement and with all the smoke, he hadn't noticed that the tribesmen had succeeded in stripping off their tops. Having already experienced Gina's unclothed breasts, he found his eyes drawn immediately to Mary Lynn's. And now, as he approached her, he couldn't help but behold their magnificence. He couldn't help but stare at them and find himself utterly transfixed by their incredible beauty. They thrust straight out from her chest with the firmness of ripe fruit—just as he'd often imagined they would—perfect and lovely, with her lightly hued nipples aroused and leading the way.

Goodness, they were beautiful. Every last succulent cell.

And just then, it occurred to him that his study was about to become credible once again, now that he would have much more data regarding Mary Lynn's unclad physique to add to his journal. Even seeing her and Gina standing side by side like this was providing him with a very clear means of comparison.

Here they were, both of them, standing right in front of him with almost nothing on.

Again, the question arose: Who was 'better,' as it were?

Gina?

Or Mary Lynn?

He recalled briefly his experience examining Gina's breasts. This had certainly overwhelmed him. Her breasts were stunning. They were arousing. They were the thing of every man's lustful dreams.

On the other hand, Mary Lynn's near nakedness was something else altogether. In this state of undress, she was beautiful in a way that he had never had occasion to observe before. She was intensely beautiful; naturally beautiful, perfectly beautiful—from head to toe.

And her curvaceous charms didn't simply arouse him. They floored him.

He swallowed hard.

But then, as he stepped before her, he was reminded of the obvious fact that this sweet and wonderful young woman was shaking like a leaf and undoubtedly scared out of her wits. Certainly, both of them were.

"Here, here, here," he said reassuringly. "Everything's okay. Everything is all right. They're gone. I shot at them again and I saw them move far out to sea before I came back here."

As he spoke, he quickly picked up Mary Lynn's torn bikini top and laid it gently over her chest, forcing his eyes to look nowhere but into hers as he did.

She smiled an almost knee-buckling smile of gratitude at him.

"They were going to take one of us to their island," she said, still breathless and still coughing. "For their king."

"He wanted one of us as a sex slave," Gina clarified.

"And they were trying to decide which one of us to take," Mary Lynn added.

"I see," he replied as he picked up Gina's top and laid it across her undulating topography. "This must have been terribly frightening for both of you."

"It most certainly was," Gina confirmed.

"It was horrific," Mary Lynn added.

"Well, let's get these vines off of both of you."

His voice was steady and reassuring, but as he bent over and picked up one of the machetes abandoned by the tribesmen, his mind was a maelstrom of conflicting energies. He knew that getting all those vines off of them — especially Mary Lynn — was going to be an awkward operation.

For both of them.

Certainly, Gina had never displayed anything even resembling modesty.

But Mary Lynn was a different matter altogether. And for that reason alone, he decided to cut her free first.

The vines were knotted together in dozens of places all over her body and he needed the machete to cut them off. But where could he do so without running the risk of cutting her?

He walked around behind her and saw that, where some of the vines stretched from her body and wrapped around the post, there were numerous areas where he could work the blade safely.

"I'll have you both free in no time, girls," he said.

And here was where the struggle taking place in his mind reached its point of no-return. As he knelt down in front of her and began cutting the vines, her indescribably gorgeous legs were now right in his face. Full, tanned and toned; he couldn't believe how beautiful they were. It was all he could do to keep from reaching out and gliding his hands up and down their lengths.

But then, as he pulled away one of the cut vines, he took one look — one brief glimpse — up into her eyes.

And she looked down at him with a look that changed everything.

It was a look that was at once shy, frightened, brave, vulnerable, and trusting.

A look that was, more than anything else, innocent.

Now, he was confused. How in the world was he to document all of her tantalizing charms when they were now overshadowed by the potentially traumatizing event which this sweet and wholesome young woman had just endured? How was he to look at her from the point of view of a healthy, vital male when he was now finding it nearly impossible to look anywhere but into her eyes?

Next, he moved behind her — feeling Gina's eyes on him every second of the way. He knelt and began to cut the next set of vines…and the next one…moving higher up…his eyes now inches from the backs of her thighs and that beautiful rear end of hers, the latter of which, of course, had been the source and subject of many moments of arousal during the past days.

In point of fact, since he'd first known her.

The marvelously curvaceous and close-up sight should have driven him mad; it should have given him a rush of sexual gratification like he never had before. But it didn't, for at that instant, his arousal at the sight of her beautiful lower half was now far outweighed by something even more powerful:

Compassion.

In an instant, the Doc's excitement at finally having the opportunity to see Mary Lynn more or less unclothed, switched directly to anger — anger at himself — for allowing himself to succumb to his curiosity and sexual urges during a most trying moment such as this.

Damn him! He had no right to even think about enjoying this, research or not. He had no right to be savoring the sight of her, no matter how titillating a sight it might have been on any other occasion. He had no right to look at her as he would a stripper when he knew full well that Mary Lynn was, in fact, the sweetest and most honorable young woman he had ever known.

From out of nowhere, his conscience spoke, or, rather, shouted:

Do what you have to do to and do it quickly!

Certainly, he could have taken full advantage of this situation. Certainly, if it had been Gina, he could very well have allowed his sex-hungry persona to enjoy the moment to the fullest. But he didn't. Not with Mary Lynn.

Mary Lynn was different.

Yes, he needed to acknowledge the fact that this was an entirely different experience than that which he'd had with Gina. Seeing her and feeling her breasts had been erotic overwhelm, adrenaline, and pure thrill. But right now, with Mary Lynn's beautiful flesh right before him, any advantage he might have taken from this situation simply felt wrong. Just plain wrong.

Do what you have to do. Quickly!

He needed to finish this.

Her hands were tied behind her back and were clasped within each other between the clefts of her soft, rounded cheeks. As he began to gently cut the vines that bound her wrists, he drew in a sharp intake of air. The view was, of course, resplendent. Clad in those bright yellow bikini bottoms, it was beyond beautiful, beyond perfect, beyond arousing. Mary Lynn had most certainly been blessed with a most amazingly beautiful rear sector. Yes, it was full and firm and exquisitely rounded. Yes, it was tantalizing. Indeed, it had been the source of countless fantasies, wonderings, and erections and now it was literally within his grasp. Mary Lynn's curvature was simply stupefying—possibly the most well-constructed piece of female flesh on the entire planet. He most certainly could have ogled the deep feminine curve at the base of each cheek, the equally breathtaking curve of their rearward protrusion, and the equally beautiful curve of her hips.

Indeed, he had every reason to allow his carnal urges to override propriety and decency.

But he didn't do it, for, although he may have had every reason, he most certainly did not have every right. Not now; not with her. Mary Lynn was too good. And this was no time for him to be bad.

More important, none of that mattered right now. What mattered was getting these vines the hell off of her!

Gently, as if reading braille, he pressed his fingertips against her soft cheek in order to push it safely away from the blade of the machete and the vines he was about to cut. But he refrained from enjoying her softness, refrained from marveling at her firmness. Instead, he simply forced his attention solely upon the machete, the vines, and her safety.

Next, moving higher, he cut the vines about her trim waist, then up her smooth bare back, finally her shoulders.

All the while, he looked closely at what he was doing—but, through sheer force of will, he looked upon her flesh with nothing but his eyes.

When he was finished, Mary Lynn quickly put her bikini top back on. Then she stepped from the post and turned to him, rubbing her arms and legs where the vines had cinched her skin. She smiled that beautiful smile of hers.

"Thank you so much, Doc." She reached up and placed a soft kiss on his cheek.

He smiled in return, and, all in all, felt pretty darned good about himself right then. He'd done the right thing. He was a man — a man with eyes and with urges — and she was a woman whom virtually every man alive would undoubtedly find indescribably gorgeous. Yet, he'd managed to set that aside and do what he'd had to do, quickly and with minimal distraction and minimal arousal.

He'd done the very best he could do under these most tempting and compelling circumstances, and he was quite proud of himself.

He smiled at her again.

She smiled back.

There was a long pause as their eyes made deep, lingering contact —

"Uh, hello! Someone's still waiting here!" Gina called out, perturbed, breaking him from his trance.

"Oh, good heavens! Of course, Gina," he said, turning toward her. "Forgive me."

And now, the Doc found himself in an entirely different experience altogether. Of course, Gina's shapely, nearly nude body was alluring as ever. Certainly, her curvaceous flesh and delicate skin were enough to make him hard and wanting — mercilessly so.

But, unlike with Mary Lynn, this time, he allowed it.

This time, he hungrily allowed himself to feast on the sight of Gina's beautiful thighs just inches from his face. He gave himself full permission to notice the velvety feel of her skin and the exquisite softness of her flesh as his hands moved everywhere upon her body. He delighted in having her meaty backside within his exhilarated grasp as he cut the vines from her. All in all, he was stimulated to the hilt by all he saw and by all he felt.

Of course, he felt bad for her, considering the ordeal she'd just been through. Of course, he worked as quickly as he could to safely free her. But at the same time, he gave himself full license to allow his masculine being to take notice of, and thoroughly enjoy, all that Gina's body had to offer.

For, if there was one thing he knew about Gina after three years together on the island it was this: Gina had no problem whatsoever with having her body taken notice of. Indeed, he knew full-well that she derived great pleasure from it.

However, the experience of freeing her was different in another way as well.

With Gina, his pleasure was confined to all the places in both his mind and body where carnal and lustful urges reside, whereas with Mary Lynn, the pleasure was located more or less everywhere *but*…and yet it somehow stimulated him more. With

Mary Lynn, he'd found himself awakened and aroused in a part of his being that he had never known before — a deeper part of himself which, even with all his intelligence and education, he couldn't name, let alone understand.

The truth of the matter was that he was now more confused than ever.

But then, just as he was cutting the last of the vines from Gina's back:

"What in the blessed name of the Seven Seas is going on here?"

There was the Captain, standing at the edge of the beach, clinging to a palm tree, teetering a bit, and looking altogether confused and disoriented.

The Doc grinned as he finished pulling the last vine away from Gina's body. Then he walked over and put his arm around his shoulder to steady him. "Cap'n, old buddy, have I got some news for you!"

* * * *

The dinnertime conversation that evening was, of course, centered around the harrowing capture and near kidnapping of Gina and Mary Lynn. Since the Captain, Finnegan, and the Powells had literally slept through the whole thing, there was much recounting to be done in order to bring everyone up to speed.

The Doc found it quite intriguing, though not the least surprising, that the other men were clearly just as interested in hearing about the women having been stripped half naked by the natives as they were the rest of the story. Even Mr. Powell was now asking an inordinate amount of questions about that particular part of the ordeal.

"And the natives actually pulled your bikini tops off?" he asked, his voice and facial expression betraying equal parts disbelief, sympathy, and arousal. "As in...completely?"

"Oh, yes," Gina replied with more than a small amount of dramatic flair. It was clear that she was enjoying seeing the men practically licking their lips at the thought. "And it was so frightful having those five young men gaping at our naked breasts, looking us up and down, and even touching our bare skin."

"And absolutely humiliating," Mary Lynn added with a blatant shudder.

Gina nodded in agreement. "Oh, yes, and I'm sure that, if the Doc hadn't come to our rescue when he did, our panties would certainly have been next. Just imagine...*me* being tied to that pole, helpless, and without one single stitch of clothing on...my entire body...exposed from head to toe...as those five young men studied me from my top to my bottom. My goodness, I'm certain that they even planned to *feel* me, as well...everywhere...all over...

my breasts, my legs...why, even my...my private parts!"

"Good heavens!" Mr. Powell gasped, eyes bulging, half rising from his seat. "And...and that means that poor Mary Lynn would have suffered the same fate, as well!"

As soon as the words were out of his mouth, he, the Captain, and Finnegan glanced over at Mary Lynn, who immediately moved her hands awkwardly, in a fidgety matter, in front of her breasts and down her front, utterly humiliated. Then they looked back at Gina, back at Mary Lynn, and back at Gina again, their lips parted ever so slightly and their eyes glazed over to an almost comical degree.

The Doc half expected to see foam coming from their mouths.

Not that he was any less aroused as he visualized, with great clarity, Gina's enhanced speculations.

But at least he wasn't being a pig about it.

* * * *

That evening, alone in his hut, the Doc wrote comprehensively on the subject of his new and altogether incomprehensible findings:

This is maddening! I don't know what to think or how to feel. When Gina bared herself to me yesterday morning so that I could examine her breasts, I was certainly sympathetic to her concern. But at the same time, I found myself in a state of complete erotic overwhelm. It was pure delight. Pure adrenaline.

Then, this afternoon, when I realized I was about to undergo a similar experience with Mary Lynn, I started off feeling equally aroused and hungry. But then, when the moment came and I could very well have delighted in her numerous feminine delights, I did not. It simply felt wrong for me to take advantage of an almost tragic experience that was clearly causing sweet, innocent Mary Lynn distress. So, I forced my attention upon the task at hand and managed to keep my male urges more or less in check.

But after another moment, I came to realize that my feelings had strayed into an altogether different and unexpected direction. Seeing this beautiful and good-hearted young woman before me — vulnerable, embarrassed, and afraid — triggered a reaction in me that seemed to emanate not from my loins, but from my entire being.

It wasn't maddening; it was peaceful; it wasn't arousing, it was redeeming.

I am at a total loss as to understanding this phenomenon.

At the same time, for reasons I can't explain, I am feeling even more reluctant to continue with my research than before — even now, after I've just been provided with very nearly equal views of each woman's female offerings. Although both women continue to arouse me and tempt me, and even though I would give anything to enjoy either one of them more 'intimately,' as it were, I am no longer feeling the same desire to speculate on and analyze them as I've been doing, or to pen commentaries about their physiques without their knowing.

Part of me wants to continue. Part of me doesn't. I simply do not know what to do next. I am utterly confused and truly at a loss...

CHAPTER EIGHT

Meanwhile, in the women's hut...

Damn those horny savages!

Gina lay silently in bed, staring up into the pitch darkness. Her lips were tight and her mind was seething at the thought.

How dare they come here and ruin everything!

It had all been going so wonderfully! She'd been doing a bang-up job of reeling the Doc in, inch by inch. Now those stupid horny natives had to show up and tie her and Mary Lynn up in their bikinis, forcing the Doc to have to come to their rescue.

And then everything went from bad to worse!

It was bad enough being abducted, tied up, stripped, and almost sent to who knows where to become some native king's sex slave. But then the Doc had to go and untie Mary Lynn and wound up with Mary Lynn's cute little picture-perfect ass right in his face while he did!

Naturally, he had to go and touch it in the process! Naturally, he had to feel it!

And, no doubt, he had himself a grand time of it, too!

Of course, he did. For goodness' sake, this wasn't just any ass, it was Mary Lynn's ass! What man *wouldn't* have thought he'd died and gone to Heaven with that well-rounded opportunity filling his eyes and hands?

The Doc—*her* Doc—with his eyes and hands all over Mary Lynn's beautiful, and woefully unbeatable ass!

It was over. She was doomed. Doomed to a life of continual loneliness and horniness.

How in heaven's name was she ever going to win him over now? No man could possibly have an experience like that with Mary Lynn's southbound goodies and be interested in anyone else from then on. There was just no way. He had her plump and perky cheeks right there in front of him, in all their semi-naked glory—Mary Lynn's goddamned perfect ass, an ass which no woman on this earth could hold a candle to, had just been all but handed to the guy. Of course, he was going to want it—and the rest of her along with it! If nothing more, the Doc wasn't blind—and he sure as hell wasn't stupid.

And, dammit, he got to ogle Mary Lynn's little tits, too! Okay, hers weren't in the same league as Gina LaPlante's, but still, they were perky as all hell and could quite possibly help to turn his head even further away from the woman who really wanted him. Besides, what if the Doc actually preferred smaller tits? Some guys were weird like that. What if he were one of them? That would just make this impossible situation all the more impossible!

Oh, god, and her thighs were right there, too! Goddammit! Mary Lynn's nifty little thighs — all smooth and shapely and right in the Doc's face.

Gina winced at the thought.

She was doomed!

This wasn't fair.

Mary Lynn with all her sweet little assets!

What could she possibly do to get the Doc's mind off all *that*?

Gina shook her head and grimaced. She'd seen the way he looked at Mary Lynn's goodies while he was cutting the vines. Sure, he'd acted all concerned and caring, but, come on, he was a guy — he must have had one hell of a hard-on the whole time, what with sweet, little Mary Lynn's bountiful booty so close he could very well have leaned forward and kissed it.

The only possibly positive thing about the whole experience was that the natives never got the chance to strip their bottoms off, too.

Mary Lynn's ass...*bare*? God, that would have been the final nail in the coffin as far as she was concerned.

But even with their bottoms on, there was Mary Lynn's tight little package — right in his ever-loving face.

Right in front of a guy who was, apparently, just now learning how to be horny!

Fucking great.

Just then, Gina wondered if Mary Lynn herself had been turned on being felt up by the Doc, emergency situation though it was. It would be just like the little farmer's daughter to ignore her prudish upbringing all of a sudden and to start developing an interest in sex — with the Doc no less — just as she, Gina LaPlante, was working her own butt off to win him over!

Gina rolled over onto her side and cuddled up more tightly against her pillow. This was terrible! Here she'd been thinking how much fun it had been to have the Doc feel her up yesterday morning. He'd been so cute, fiddling and fumbling with her lovin' handfuls and stammering like a schoolboy the whole time. And it had felt so good to finally feel a man's hands on her, even it was under rather false pretenses. Still, it was clear to her, even from those few innocent touches, that she wanted the Doc more than ever and she wanted him now.

Gina's face was now creased with worry. But what if the Doc liked Mary Lynn better now? And what if Mary Lynn were to up and decide that she'd enjoyed being felt up by him so much that she wanted more of it — and him? Here she was thinking that the Doc was all hers and then Mary Lynn winds up with the golden opportunity to get captured, stripped by the natives, and then groped to High Heaven by the Doc!

Her Doc!

Gina sighed sad and long. She loved Mary Lynn; she really did. But she certainly wanted the Doc more than her hut-mate did; she was sure of it. And she simply couldn't stomach the thought of losing her chance to get it on with him.

Whether Mary Lynn flaunted it or not, her sweet and perfect ass was one tough competitor.

Well, she could be tougher! As far as she was concerned, the Doc was all hers. If Mary Lynn's sex-drive were to kick in anytime soon, she would just have to content herself with one of the other available bachelors on this island!

No doubt about it, she needed to take things to the next level with her man of science. Even after having his way with Mary Lynn's killer keister, he still must have thoroughly enjoyed squeezing *her* luscious tittie for those few minutes, hadn't he? And certainly, he must have enjoyed pressing his fingers against her lady goodies as he cut *her* vines off as well, hadn't he? Well, he damned well better have! She knew of plenty of men who would gladly have paid her upwards of a thousand dollars for the very same teat-treats that the Doc had been granted — for free! If he had half a brain and half a cock, he simply *had* to be hungry for more.

But should she go after him tonight? Or might that scare him off? Should she amuse herself for the time being with little beyond offering him more eye candy and perhaps another opportunity to feel her up?

Skinny-dipping and 'forgetting' how to swim?

Fake nude sleepwalking into his hut?

A pelvic exam?

No! Mary Lynn's ass was a major threat — one that needed to be nipped in the butt. This was going to happen and it was going to happen tonight. It was for his own good as well as hers. He sure as hell needed it and so did she. And, judging by his voluntary presence at the waterfall with his trusty binoculars, as well as his turning her simple little breast exam from what would normally be less than a minute into a feel-up that was five times longer and which left telltale evidence on his pants, he clearly had desire for her!

It was settled, then. Tonight, she would end her three long years of chastity and give the Doc a sorely needed lesson on the subject of sex a-la Gina!

* * * *

Gina lay quietly in her bed for several long minutes until she was certain that Mary Lynn was in a good sound sleep. Once her roommate's breathing was deep and steady, she slipped out of bed and into her white beaded dress that had 'fuck me, sweetheart' just written all over it. It was low cut and very form-fitting. In fact, it was the best presentation of her goodies that she had, short of walking in on him stark naked. Just before leaving, she spritzed on some perfume, brushed her hair until it was soft, silky, and grabbable, then deepened the pink of her lips with some island-berry lipstick. After giving herself a sexy smile of approval in her mirror, she tiptoed out of the hut and over to the Doc's.

She noted with a satisfied smile, even at this late hour, that his was the only one with any light shining from within.

She tapped on the bamboo door.

"Come in?"

This was it. She took a deep breath, opened the door, and stepped inside.

There he was, seated at his table, scribbling in his diary as if he had a deadline to meet, his face beautifully lit by the light of three candles. He looked up and smiled.

"Gina!" he said softly. "What are you doing up and about at this hour?"

She could tell from the up-down he gave her that he'd consciously omitted the words: *dressed like that.*

She smiled her warmest, most sensual smile, then slinked over to stand before him. "Oh, I couldn't sleep and I was afraid of waking Mary Lynn. I saw your light and thought you might like some company."

He looked quizzically at her, then, once again, dropped his gaze down her body. "Company? Why...yes, of course. That would be...very nice." He tore his eyes away from her and looked about the hut. "I'm afraid I don't have another chair to offer..."

She shrugged. "Oh, that's all right. May I just sit on your bed?"

Or on your face, sweetie?

His mouth opened and closed a few times. "My bed? Why...yes, of course. Please...sit down, won't you?"

She smiled, then walked to the side of his bunk and sat down, her eyes feigning brief interest in all the trappings of his living space: his books, his clothing locker, his razor and other grooming supplies, his table full of bamboo test tubes and other scientific bric-a-brac. Then she looked at him and found him watching her with male interest which he'd clearly failed to disguise.

That was all the encouragement she needed.

She leaned back slightly on her arms, giving him a succulent view of her statuesque, six-foot form. Then she made the view even more compelling by casually tilting her head back and thrusting her pelvis forward just a touch. As soon as she did, his mouth opened and his eyes shot straight toward her woman spot for just an instant before he forced them back onto his journal.

"So…what are writing about?" she asked with feigned interest.

"Oh…just making corrections and annotations in my catalog of the various tropical birds on this island. I've been studying the beautiful Mynah bird lately, in fact. A most fascinating creature. In fact, did you know that a male and female Mynah will mate for life?"

"Ooh, that sounds fascinating, Doc." She stood and walked back to where he sat. "May I see?"

Whatever it takes…

"Why…yes, of course. That is, if you're interested in such things."

Oh, of course, I am," she lied, then bent over to read from his journal, all the while doing her best to position her bawdy, beaded butt as close to his face as she could.

She could practically feel his unsteady breath on her cheek.

Gina pretended to skim his notes, then flipped through a few pages.

"Wow, Doc, it's just so amazing that you can do all this. I've always been in such awe of you and your keen analytical mind." She bent further and turned slightly, allowing her right cheek to press firmly and lingeringly against his shoulder.

She started to turn some more pages —

But just then, the Doc hurriedly slid the book from her grasp and closed it. She looked up and saw a look of near-panic cross his face briefly.

"What's wrong, Doc?"

His mouth opened and closed again. "Oh, well...it's just that...it's just that it gets even more boring the further you —" His gaze shifted for several delicious seconds over to her ass, then back to her face. "The, um, further you go."

Like it? You can go as far as you want with my *tushy, honey.*

She nodded. "Ah, I see." Frankly, his response towards her wanting to read his journal was pretty darned strange. Still, she did her best to not let it distract her from her mission.

Seconds later, she looked deep into his eyes. "Can I ask you a question, Doc?"

He breathed a sigh of relief. "Why, of course, you can, Gina."

A faint smile teased her lips. "I've been wondering...do scientists — well, do they have the same thoughts and feelings as regular men?"

He appeared surprised by her question. "Why...yes, of course, we do. I mean, I'm quite sure that we do."

"What I mean is, do scientists have... *romantic* thoughts like regular men?" While she spoke, she maneuvered her prized titties into his field of vision for added emphasis.

His eyes leaped forward, drinking in the sight for a brief but very telling moment. He definitely liked what he saw, she could tell. He'd sure liked them yesterday morning when he was squeezing the bejeezus out of them.

"I...I'm sure we do, Gina," he stammered, his eyes opening wider.

She leaned forward and captured them with hers, peering straight into his soul so deep that he literally began to squirm.

"Does that include you?" she asked in a husky whisper.

The Doc's mouth opened and closed a half-dozen times. "Well, I...um...I...I mean, perhaps... on rare occasion..."

"So, have you ever, you know, made love to a woman?"

The Doc's mouth opened and closed a dozen more times. Then: "Oh, forgive me. What an inconsiderate host I've been! Here I am, inviting you inside my hut and not even offering you a drink.

Would you like some pineapple juice?" He all but jumped from his chair and began backing shakily toward the door. "That would be nice, wouldn't it? It's so refreshing on warm nights like this. I—I'll be...right back."

He turned and practically leaped from the hut.

A wicked smile spread slowly across her face. "That's a 'no'," she said softly.

So, the Doc was a virgin. Just as she'd thought. Well, this was going to be piece of cake, wasn't it? That is, as long as he didn't come *too* quickly!

Just then, she glanced down and saw the journal lying on the table. Then she recalled his panicked reaction a moment ago, when she'd tried to flip through it, and the thought made her curious to find out what was inside that would have caused him to get so worked up about her seeing it.

Casting a brief glimpse toward the door, she slid the journal over, opened it, and began flipping pages.

Ten seconds later, her eyes leaped onto a page that was divided into two columns—with Mary Lynn's and her name written at the top of each! "What the...?"

She skimmed the ensuing pages quickly for a few illuminating minutes. Then, after reading for as long as she dared, she closed it to await his return.

"Well, well, well," she crooned. "Fascinating research. 'Who's more anatomically equipped,' huh? 'Who's more able to satisfy a man sexually?'" She pursed her lips. "Well, I do believe this hot researcher is about to find out!"

Thinking fast, she brought her thumbs and forefingers up to her breasts, down inside her bra, and began squeezing her nipples hard and fast — wincing, gasping, and grinning the whole time — making them all nice and hard for him. She continued her assault until she heard his footsteps outside.

Then the door opened and he came in carrying two tall bamboo cups. He smiled and held one out to her. Gina simply took it — and his as well — and set them on the table. Then, before he could say a word, she turned toward him and brought her plump, wet lips against his.

His eyes opened wide.

She pulled him into her arms and went at him again.

She began sucking his lower lip, then his upper. Then she thrust her skillful tongue between them with everything she had, bathing his hot tongue with hers in slow circular strokes.

Here's some more data for your research, darling. My treat.

His eyes opened wider still.

She moved her hands across his back, caressing him in every way—romantically, sensually, erotically. She massaged his shoulder blades, she caressed his back, she explored his thighs, she groped his nifty butt—every move she made causing him to flinch, shudder, or gasp...much to her exquisite pleasure.

Then...lo and behold! He began to follow her lead. Soon his two strong hands were moving across the expanse of *her* back, her thighs, and *her* bottom—and, oh, did it ever feel delicious!

Mmm, yes...so very nice!

And she was oh-so happy that his hands seemed thrilled with *her* cheeks filling them up now, instead of Mary Lynn's!

More and more she used her lips—her very talented and insured-for-$50,000 lips—on him. On his mouth, on his neck, on his ears.

He moaned.

She moaned in reply.

She returned her mouth to his.

Her tongue began thrusting hard against his.

He thrust his in return, fast learner that he was.

She sucked and drew his tongue deep into her mouth, then let him do the same.

He squeezed her ass harder, at first tentatively, then more audaciously.

She returned the gesture with a hard, fast grab of his wide-awake cock that elicited a sound from somewhere deep inside him that was a gratifying blend of gasp, moan, groan, and seizure.

Mm-hm...even nicer!

Finally, she brought her legendary bod right up against him, grinding her pelvis against his, luxuriating in the feeling of his hardness against her softness. Mmm, yes, he was getting nicely primed now!

Licking, sucking, tonguing, squeezing—right there in the middle of the hut, lit only by candles, a sultry tropical breeze wafting in, a beautiful movie star in his arms—Gina was certain that his first real contact with a woman would never be forgotten.

A moment later, she pulled away from him, but her eyes and lips remained close.

"Unzip me," she ordered, her murmuring voice practically menacing.

"Wha—?"

"I *said* unzip me."

Panic shot into his voice. "Gina, I, um..." Then, with sudden concern: "Oh, my, is it your breasts again?"

She smiled and shook her head, then reached back, unzipped her dress, and let it fall to the floor, her eyes never leaving his. The Doc looked down at it briefly, then back at her, his eyes just about ready to go into cardiac arrest.

"Yes, Doc, it *is* my breasts again." She reached back and began to unclasp her lace-trimmed bra. "Poor little things. They've definitely been in need of special treatment lately."

She pulled it off by the cups and let it fell to the floor atop her dress. The Doc's eyes followed its descent all the way, then returned to the soft, supple, twin protrusions that awaited him.

Here, dear, here are a couple more items to stick in your journal...

She took two steps toward him.

The Doc was visibly shaking now as he stared at her breasts, his eyes honed in onto her well-pinched and very swollen nipples. She, too, glanced down at them and smiled seductively.

"Y-y-you mean, you want me to examine them again?"

Her smile widened and she shook her head once again. "I want you to *suck* them, Doc. I want you to put them between your beautiful lips and suck them like they're the two best lollipops you ever tasted." She pressed them against his chest, moving her naked flesh in slow circles against him.

"Well, I...I...I...I—"

"Suck them," she crooned directly into his ear. "Come on, lover boy. Suck my tits. You can do it. I'm sure it will do them—and each of us—a world of good."

Slowly, and without a word, the Doc bent forward. Then he took her right breast in his hand, hefting it, squeezing it softly. Finally, he raised it to his mouth and brought his open lips against its surface.

Gina's head shot toward the ceiling and she squealed. It was such an innocent move, really, especially compared to the way these very same tits had been ravaged by producers over the years. Still, considering how long it had been since those lusty days, it was nonetheless a shocking sensation that immediately moistened her panties.

"The nipple, Doc. Suck it. Hard. Come on, you'll love it, I promise. I've been told many times that they're very tasty."

He looked up at her as if in a trance, then lowered his head again and took her very swollen and nearly bruised right nipple between his lips and began to suck her, first gently, then harder. First awkwardly, then more masterfully.

Yes, indeed, a very quick learner, he was.

"*Ooooh!*" she whispered, grinning. "Yes, that's it, darling, you're doing fine...a little harder...that's it...now the other one."

He obeyed, his mouth hopping quickly to her left twin.

"That's it...*mmm*...that's it, honey. Keep doing that. Oooh, yes, that's great...*aah*...now lick it, too...now flick it with your tongue...now give it a tiny, tiny little bite."

The Doc followed her instructions to the letter.

She gasped once more, then perhaps ten more times after that. Then: "So...do you like them?"

He nodded, then, still sucking away, mumbled, "Your breasts are...um...beautiful. And, yes, quite tasty as well."

She smiled broadly. "Why, thank you. But call them 'tits'. I want to hear you talk like that."

"Um, y-y-your tits are beautiful, Gina."

"*Mmm*...that's good to hear, Doc." She took his hand from her left breast and pulled it down to her moist panties. "Rub me here at the same time," she breathed. "It's delightful down there, too. Very tropical. A dark, mysterious jungle to get lost in...and oh-so warm and humid."

"Why, um, yes, of...of course."

And that was that. No sooner did his fingers begin to rub and caress her lips, Gina let out a moan to end all moans.

"*Uunnhh!*" Then: "Ooh, yes, that's it, Doc! That's it. Faster...yes, like that!" Then: "Here...rub here...no, no...higher...a little higher." She moved his frantic fingers up to her swollen love nub. "Right there...rub it good!"

Then: "*Uunnnhhhh!*"

The Doc was still sucking on her nipple and his fingers were quickly becoming more skillful in their new occupation. Gina began tossing her head from side to side and bucking her hips forward and back.

"*Ooh*! That's-it-that's-it-that's-it that's-it! Oh, god! Yes-yes-yes-yes-*yeeesss*!"

She was losing it. She was losing control. It had been so, so very long and she was so, so horny.

She couldn't wait any longer. She wanted him now. She needed him *now*!

Suddenly, she pulled both her breast from his mouth and his hand from her pussy. Then, before he could say a word, she ripped his white shirt from his chest, sending buttons flying about the hut. His pants and shorts followed suit in very short order.

And that only made things worse, for her when she took a good, long look at his shockingly smooth and well-proportioned body, she all but lost it again. He had a beautiful, hairless chest, a taut stomach, and thighs that sure would feel good straddling her. His cock was just a tad on the slender side, but what it lacked in girth it made up for in classic, clean-lined beauty. In any case, he was one well-built hunk of man, that was for sure.

"Holy, ever-loving god...get your butt over here right now." She yanked him over to his bunk and lay down, spreading her legs as wide as the

Pacific.

"Get inside me. Quick! I need you in here, Doc! I need you inside me!" Her voice was growing louder, more frantic, and more commanding by the second. She was losing her mind. She knew she was, but she was far too revved up by now to care. "Hurry up! Come inside me! Now!"

"Why, um, yes, of...of course, Gina." With somewhat less enthusiasm than she'd expected, he walked to the end of the bunk, knelt down gingerly on the edge, and poised himself before her. Then, awkward as a nun at a bachelor party, he maneuvered himself between her legs and brought his cock right up to her lurching lips.

Then he paused.

Gina stared at him.

"Um, now?" he inquired.

"Yes, goddammit. Now. Get in here. Fuck me. Come on. Fuck me hard, Doc. All the way, Doc. Come on. If we're going to be stuck on this island for a while, let's at least have a blast together!"

With no fanfare, whatsoever, the Doc simply did as he was told. He slipped inside her and began to move...tentatively...instinctively.

The instant he was fully embedded inside her, Gina exploded.

"*Ooooooooohhhhhh! Do-o-o-oc!*" She couldn't help it. Three torturous years of waiting and her hugely frustrated sexual muse was finally granted parole. God, did it ever feel good having his firm length thrusting within and against her feminine innards! Did it ever feel grand having her hungry lips squeeze themselves tightly around him! As she continued to cry out and pant, she began thrashing wildly on the bunk, bucking her hips and grasping frantically at his chest. "Fuck me!" she growled. "Come on, Doc. Harder. *Harder*. Keep going!"

Her brand-new lover did as he was told.

"Come on, Doc, I want you deeper than that...that's it. And I want you to suck on my tits some more."

He thrust. He sucked. And he did both with a sort of forceful determination she found surprising but also quite enjoyable.

"Ooh, yeah! Like that!"

Barely a moment later: "Now I want you to squeeze my ass, too."

He obeyed, grasping and groping every inch of her cheeks as if memorizing them, at one point even grazing hesitantly across her anus with the back of a single timid but curious finger.

She squealed and shuddered from the sensation of his daring exploration. "Ooh, that's it. Yes, squeeze it some more. Touch it some more. It's nice, isn't it?" He nodded absently. Then: "You do like my ass, don't you, Doc? I mean, it's certainly better than *most*, isn't it?"

He nodded again, breathless as he continued to partake of her flouncing buns with both his hands. "Yes, Gina, it's...um...very nice, indeed. Very pliable, very well-proportioned, symmetrical, and resilient."

Oh, for crying out loud!

"That's good, darling," she whispered. "Feel away all you want. I want you to enjoy yourself. And just think: How many men can say they got to have sex with a gorgeous movie star like me *and* got to suck her tits and feel her ass at the same time, right?"

He nodded, still thrusting, still sucking, still squeezing.

Within seconds, she started coming again. All over the place. She came and she went and she came again, whimpering and calling out the whole time. Yes! This is precisely what she'd needed for so, so long! "Fuck me, Doc!" she yelped, somehow aware that everyone on the island could easily hear her, but unable and unwilling to do anything about it at the moment.

"That's it, baby...*oooh*...yes! Keep sucking my tits...*mmm*...yes, yes, yes! Come on, keep going...keep going...harder...faster...deeper. Keep doing it...keep doing all of it!"

The Doc did everything he was told, slamming himself into her and gasping softly the whole time. He glided and thrust and Gina thrust right back at him. Like an animal, she flounced upon the bed, lifting her legs straight toward the ceiling, then resting them upon his shoulders, moaning, whimpering, calling out. It was too incredible a sensation to do anything less.

Three years had taken its toll on her.

Yes…this was good. It was so very good.

But after another minute or so, Gina realized that, although the Doc seemed to be enjoying himself well enough, there was nothing in the way of that all-consuming rapture typical of a virgin's first time, especially a virgin who was doing it with *the* Gina LaPlante. Hell, she was enjoying it more than him! What could possibly be the matter with him?

And even when he came, scarcely a minute later, it was almost an anti-climax. He simply groaned, shuddered, and came—in all of six or seven seconds.

Then it was over. Panting, he withdrew from her, rolled onto his back, and lay quietly, staring vacantly at the ceiling as his breathing slowed.

Gina waited for him to speak, to compliment her, to say something—anything!

But he didn't. Finally, she just had to ask: "Doc? Did you enjoy that? Did you enjoy me?"

He blinked back to reality. "Oh, um, why, yes, it was…it was wonderful, Gina. A truly gratifying and enjoyable experience, indeed."

Gina sighed inwardly. That was a 'no.' One thing was for certain: The Doc was a terrible liar and a lousy actor. What in heaven's name was going on, she wondered for the first of many times that night.

CHAPTER NINE

Breakfast the next morning was an awkward affair, to say the least. Even while keeping his head lowered and his eyes glued to his pineapple and turtle eggs, the Doc could literally feel the stares and glares from everyone as he ate. Peeking up from time to time, he could also see that Gina was receiving the very same types of looks: The Captain looked angry and jealous, Finnegan looked frustrated and even more jealous, Mary Lynn looked confused and hurt, Mrs. Powell appeared aghast, and Mr. Powell, a strange combination of appalled and intrigued. Considering the volume of Gina's piercing vocalizations last night, it was obvious that they'd all heard every last lusty syllable. Mercifully, no one said a word to either of them. In fact, no one said a word to anyone. They all simply ate, stared, hurried through their meal, and then couldn't seem to go their separate ways quickly enough.

He sighed with relief, then quickly retreated to the sanctity of his hut for a much-needed journal session.

It was certainly not at all what I expected, to be honest. Gina is such a wonderful and beautiful woman and when she undressed in front of me, and I was invited to touch her so intimately, I was understandably and greatly "turned on," as they say. I would certainly have added very high marks in my science journal for her wonderful and shapely physique. Her breasts were absolutely splendid...even more so than when I first beheld them. Her nipples were swollen into a very alluring proportion and more deeply hued this time. I am left to wonder if perhaps this was somehow connected to her level of arousal.

In any event, I thoroughly enjoyed viewing and caressing her stunning curves and glorious softness. I was in awe that I was even permitted such liberties with a celebrity of her beauty and renown.

And yet...

I'm almost sorry to even admit this, especially given my level of arousal at the onset, but after a few brief moments of rapture and thrill, I found my desire quickly ebbing.

Indeed, as events unfolded, I found my arousal all but extinguished by Gina's behavior. I found that even her physical allure could not compensate for the way in which she became a) very demanding of me, and b) rather savage in her behavior. It was disquieting and not terribly arousing to me. Furthermore, it lacked any semblance of romance or sensuality whatsoever.

It all left me dazed and quite confused, not to mention tired and sore. On one hand, I should be thankful for my first ever sexual congress — with a beautiful and desirable woman no less. But on the other hand, I felt that there was so much that was missing from the experience, though I cannot seem to determine what that 'something' is.

And the worst part of the experience is this aftermath I now find myself in. I have been given full access to experience the degree of sexual allure and skill of one subject and not the other. There is, after all, no way I would ever be granted a comparable experience with a woman like Mary Lynn.

And this very fact leaves my research at a standstill, for it is unlikely that I will never really know the answer to the question of which woman is "better," as it were.

I must confess that it was all a poorly conceived project from the start and should, therefore, be shelved indefinitely.

Furthermore, deep in my heart, I believe I already know what the ultimate outcome of my study would have been…

He paused and stared off into space for a moment as a barrage of brand-new thoughts and feelings overcame him. Thoughts and feelings powerful enough to confuse, astound, and overwhelm him. He sighed deeply and sadly, then continued to write.

Finally, after several more minutes, he stopped, pondered his situation briefly, and flipped back to the science section of his journal.

"Perhaps it's time I resumed my real work once again," he said with quiet determination. "Perhaps this time my attention will remain uncompromised and I will remain on-task."

Without another thought, he stood, snatched the journal and pen off the table, threw them and his binoculars into his knapsack, and headed out once again in search of the Mynah bird.

Exactly as he should have been doing all along.

* * * *

Working as quickly as she could, and asking no help from anyone, Mary Lynn finished clearing the table and washing the dishes, all the while wanting nothing better than to get herself as far away from everyone as she could. She kept her head down and her gaze averted, making it clear to anyone who might happen by that she was in no mood to chat. Then, as soon as the coast was clear, she slipped away from the clearing and walked into the jungle, heading in no particular direction.

The destination didn't matter; all she wanted was to be alone.

She was so confused she didn't know what to think, or, indeed, even where she was going. Her path simply wound its way through the jungle to some as-yet-undetermined point on the far side of the island. She cared not in the least where she ended up, so long she was far enough out of sight to avoid having anyone inquire about the look of upset that must certainly be written all over her face.

Those sounds last night—Gina's howling and her screamed obscenities, the Doc's moaning and obvious delirium from having his way with a beautiful and sexy movie star—all of them continued to echo in her mind. Over and over she replayed them as she walked quickly through the lush jungle growth. Normally, she would have kept her eyes open for butterflies to admire or a beautiful tropical flower to put in her hair. Normally, the ceaseless serenading of the tropical songbirds would have intrigued and entertained her. But right now, she saw only the path and heard only those sounds from last night as they replayed ceaselessly in her imagination.

She was confused, all right, and her emotions were in a tizzy. First and foremost, she was angry at Gina and not even sure why. So, she'd made love with the Doc...so what? They were both consenting adults and she wasn't in charge of either one of them. Same for the Doc. Yes, she liked him very much and found him to be a very handsome and wonderful man. But she herself certainly had no intention of seducing him — if, in fact, she even knew how. Besides, the Doc had just made love to a glamorous, well-endowed Hollywood star. He certainly wouldn't be interested in making advances toward a simple farmgirl from Homer's Corners, Kansas.

She slowed, staring off absently into the distance. But, oh, wouldn't it have been wonderful if he had! Even though she'd been scared out of her mind the day before, when she and Gina had been captured by the natives, she couldn't deny the fact that having felt the Doc's strong hands all over her bare skin as he untied her had enticed and aroused her in ways she hadn't even known existed. And even though it had mortified her when that tribesman had ripped off the top of her bikini and stared hungrily at her bare breasts, she was less embarrassed having the Doc see her that way than she would if anyone else had come to her rescue. Truthfully, having him see her had even titillated her, for goodness' sake. She wondered what that could possibly mean. Was it having heard Gina go on the other day about how much she enjoyed having men see her nude? No, this was something else altogether. It was something that, in the end, made her feel good — womanly even — certainly not tawdry.

What's more, hearing Gina talk about the Doc and how charming and handsome he was had brought to light faint feelings she'd had for him ever since they were marooned. She'd always been attracted to him. She'd often wondered what he was really like as a man. She'd occasionally dreamt of him taking her in his arms and bathing her lips with his, then lying her down and making sweet, passionate love to her. Yes, it was true: she'd had an unspoken 'thing' for the Doc for nearly three years now — an attraction that had secretly tantalized her and even made her toy with the remote possibility that he had feelings for her, as well.

Until Miss High-and-Mighty Movie Star just up and decided that *she* wanted him and, well, when it came to men, whatever Gina wanted, Gina got. What was the use in her even thinking about going up against a woman like her?

She felt the strangest sensation as she continued walking, nearing the beach on the east end of the island. It was an overwhelming blend of confusion, jealousy, outrage, desire, and sadness that felt altogether unpleasant and made her head spin. It was quickly overwhelming her ability to think straight. It was also beginning to stir up powerful sensations 'down there' whenever her imagination began to conjure up scenes of the Doc lying on top of *her* instead of Gina.

Now she was even more confused.

A few minutes later, she began to see white sand peeking through the last remaining palm and coconut trees on the path. This was her favorite beach on the island. Small and welcoming, ensconced within the fold of two matching hillsides and offering a stunning view of the ocean as well as several tiny uninhabited islets that dotted the horizon like so many green goosebumps. She smiled at the familiar, welcoming sight and quickened her pace as she approached it.

Fifty yards further, the jungle opened up to the beach and Mary Lynn stepped out onto the soft, soothing sand, kicking off her sandals along the way. It was low tide and the narrow beach extended another fifty yards to the water. She walked half the distance, then simply sat down, resting her elbows on her knees, and stared out at the sea.

But the longer she sat, the less she noticed the rhythmic pounding of the surf and the more she heard the sounds of Gina...the Doc...Gina...the Doc...her squealing...his moaning...

Her feeling of overwhelm was increasing. Between the sights and sounds that she couldn't clear out of her head, the collage of emotions they were creating, and the resulting shudders and stirrings springing up deep inside her, she was a basket case.

Suddenly, she stood and began pacing from one end of the beach to the other, just walking aimlessly and in circles to try and clear her head and expend some of this overpowering sexual energy of hers.

Round and round she went, moving closer and closer to the water's edge.

Minutes later, her meandering brought her ankle deep into the water. The coolness snapped her mind out of its perseveration and back to the present moment. Immediately she noticed the beauty surrounding her and the refreshing tingle of the water. It felt so good and it really was the perfect cooldown. She ventured deeper, first to her calves, then to her knees. Yes, this was just what she needed. Raising the hem of her gingham dress higher, she ventured further.

Yes, this was so very nice. She smiled her first deep smile of the day and began to twirl around in the water, letting it cool her thighs, which, conveniently, were not far from the part of her that needed cooling the most.

Around and around she twirled, losing herself completely in the experience. Otherwise, she might have seen the one particularly enormous wave that swept up behind her without warning and came crashing down upon her, pushing her down below the surface and sweeping her toward the shore.

Her head popped up above the surface a few seconds later. Coughing and laughing, she got to her feet and waded out of the water and back onto dry sand.

She was drenched from head to toe. Her gingham dress now clung to her body from top to bottom, and, although the air was in the upper-80s, her teeth began chattering within seconds.

Without missing a beat, Mary Lynn looked from side to side, making sure no one was around, as she walked over to the edge of the jungle. There she made short work of peeling off her sopping wet dress, bra, and panties, wringing them out, and then draping them over a bush to dry in the warm tropical breeze.

This wasn't the first time she'd found herself nude on this beach. She'd secretly skinny-dipped here many times, in fact — beginning with the time Gina had teased her for having never done so. But those were always under the cover of darkness or dusk and, of course, her body was safely hidden below the surface of the water. This was the first time she'd ever taken off all her clothes and remained in full view on the beach in broad daylight. Although she knew that virtually no one else ever came out here, and that she was as alone as she could possibly be, she couldn't help feeling just a bit daring — and a bit naughty.

She sat down, right there on the edge of the jungle, her nudity at least partially hidden within the shade of the low-hanging palm leaves and tropical plants. But she didn't stay there long, for as the ocean breezes blew across her wet skin, she found herself chilled to the bone in minutes. Shivering, she stood and walked quickly out from the shade and back onto the middle of the beach. Here she chose a spot to relax that was directly facing into the warming sun.

At first, she knelt demurely, shielding her body from view as much as she could. Then, ten seconds later, she couldn't help laughing. Who, after all, was she shielding her body from? The songbirds? The fish? The thought relaxed her and she decided to stretch out on the sand and just drink in the sun, letting it shine brightly upon her chilled, damp, and very naked body.

She soon found it intriguing how lying here with nothing on brought her attention to her body so acutely. She felt the sun and the breeze caress her skin from head to toe and it made her feel more sensual than ever. She felt the sun and the breeze on her breasts and delighted in the tingling that resulted from the drying-up droplets of water on them. She felt the sun and the breeze between her legs and couldn't decide whether all those tingling sensations left her feeling more touched or more caressed.

She smiled. Either way, it all felt so good — strange, but good.

Feeling her body exposed to the air also caused her to once again recall the day before, when the Doc had had his strong and gentle hands on her bare skin as he cut the vines from her. When she had felt him press his hands and fingers against her stomach, her back, her thighs, her hips, and her bottom, it had felt so intimate—so intimately arousing—even with the echoes of fear still reverberating through her. Indeed, it was his touch upon her skin that had provided her first measure of calm following the horrifying ordeal of their capture. No man had ever touched her in all those places before. Except for Jimmy Johnson, no man had ever touched her intimately in any way whatsoever. And for it to have been someone as charming, handsome, and virile as the Doc made for a most intoxicating memory.

Indeed, it was a thrill she knew she would never forget.

Unfortunately, these erotic sensations also brought up images of the Doc and Gina once again. The dreamy smile fell from her lips as she imagined them together. He'd probably kissed her and she, him. Passionately, no doubt. With tongues, of course. They'd probably had all their clothes off. Perhaps the Doc had touched and caressed Gina's fabulous nude body. He certainly must have enjoyed that. Perhaps Gina had touched his as well.

Had he run his fingers through her hair, she wondered. Had he caressed her neck and shoulders? Had he brought his hands onto those big, beautiful breasts of hers? Had he trailed his fingers down the length of her legs? Had he touched her — her — ?

She squeezed her eyes shut at the thought.

And had the Doc lain right on top of Gina, his lean, masculine body pressed into her, his handsome face grazing hers as he — as he — ?

Now she winced. Damn it! Why should Gina alone have the right to make love with any and every man she wanted?

And even more maddening: why should she, Mary Lynn Saunders, have been raised with such old-fashioned morals and, therefore, developed the kind of goody-goody personality that kept her from being with boys more often than the handful of times that she'd had? Why couldn't she have been at least a little like Gina? Why couldn't she have decided, even against her upbringing, to have acted at least a little flirtier, a little more daring, and a little sexier when in the company of men?

If she had, maybe it would have been her in the Doc's hut last night instead of Gina.

Maybe it would have been she who would have made advances to him, or at least elicited and welcomed advances from him. Maybe it would have been she who would have stood there in his hut as he pressed his lips to hers…and slowly pressed his tongue between them...and brought his fingers through her hair...and caressed her shoulders. And maybe then he would have brought his hands onto her breasts and stroked them gently — or maybe not so gently. Maybe he would have brought his hands behind her, caressed her shoulders, and then moved down the length of her back to squeeze her bottom affectionately — or maybe even lustily. And maybe, just maybe, he would have dared to bring his hand audaciously down between her legs as they stood kissing.

Lord, that would have felt wonderful; she was certain of it. And maybe he would have thought it felt wonderful as well...

Her...the Doc...together intimately...

The Doc...with his tongue sliding across hers...

The Doc...touching her, caressing her... everywhere...

The Doc...easing his body on top of hers...sliding lovingly inside her...

Slowly, very slowly, and without even realizing it at first, Mary Lynn's right-hand fingers dipped into her mouth, then moved down to the juncture of her thighs. Then...she brought her knees up and allowed them to spread apart.

Finally, she brought her fingers to the place where her womanly lips were already open to the breeze and open to the sun. Both powers of nature now flowed right inside her, causing sensations that positively entranced her. Never before had she felt anything so frighteningly delicious. She grazed her outer lips gently with her fingers, bringing their wetness onto her virgin flesh, then eased them inside, where she encountered even more wetness and still more pleasure.

Her...the Doc...together intimately.

Suddenly, she arched her back, momentarily raising her bottom from the sand in response to a powerful contraction from within.

In her mind, the Doc was using his fingers, lips, and tongue on her in much the same way. She imagined him discovering her most sensitive areas. She imagined him using his thumb and fingers to gently separate her quivering virgin lips. She imagined his lips...his tongue...his hot breath... all...right there.

She arched again...and then again...and she even began to moan quietly as the waves continued their plundering of the beach right beside her.

* * * *

The Doc stooped down beside the stream and enjoyed a few handfuls of cool water. Then he stood and turned from side to side, trying to decide which jungle path to take next. He wiped sweat from his brow. He shooed a fly away. Seconds later, he nodded decisively and chose the path that wound its way toward the east beach.

Within an hour after starting out, he had already covered much of the dense section of the jungle that took up much of the eastern half of the island in his search for the elusive Mynah bird couple, whose apparently first sexual encounter he'd missed out on the day before. The reason for his rapid progress was obvious: Today, he was simply walking and not paying attention to island wildlife whatsoever. He hadn't paused to study a single bird dropping. He'd lifted no leaves to check the underside for insect eggs. He'd crouched behind no rocks to examine moss.

He was simply moving and that was all.

Despite the oppressive heat and humidity in the jungle, he walked quickly. It felt damned good to be out here alone, at least trying to do his work again. Furthermore, he certainly welcomed any opportunity to expend some energy and hopefully clear his head from the barrage of curvaceous distractions, sexual preoccupations, erotic ruminations, and outright obsessions on the subject of women that had taken possession of all his faculties lately, particularly since the night before...

At least until the path came to an abrupt end, opening up onto the island's small easternmost beach, the one he'd been to only a handful of times throughout the last three years. It had never held much appeal to him really; the ocean that abutted it was too rough to invite as many species of wildlife as the other beaches were. Here there was little more than sand.

He was just about to turn around and head in a different direction when he realized that today the beach held more than just sand.

Much more.

CHAPTER TEN

The Doc drew in a sharp breath. There was Mary Lynn, lying completely nude upon the sand, not forty feet away, her legs spread apart, her right hand wildly stroking her — good heavens! — her womanly orifice and her left hand pinching her — good heavens! –her nipples!

His mouth opened wide. So much for escaping his sexual preoccupations.

He wanted to turn away, but he couldn't.

He didn't want to look at her, but he looked just the same.

He knew that it was wrong for him to watch, but the entire scene was just too compellingly beautiful to turn away from. The spellbinding silhouette of Mary Lynn's body against the white sand, her curves, her skin, her fluttering hair, her pose, her movements — they were so beautiful, so innocent and yet so wildly enticing. In this time and place, he was seeing a Mary Lynn who he'd never known and never even imagined. He had never seen her—indeed, any woman—ever look so alluring.

Truth be told, she was the most beautiful woman he'd ever seen in his life.

His breathing increased and he found himself growing aroused almost immediately.

Again, he considered leaving, but he was simply too entranced to do anything save continue to drink in the sight of her. Indeed, after a few more seconds, he even dared to take one step closer.

One fatal step.

It was a careless step that caused him to brush against the branch of a tree, the movement frightening the very pair of Mynah birds he'd been searching for right out of the nest they'd built there. Up and out they darted, swooping over Mary Lynn and screeching wildly as they shot up the hillside to his left and out of sight.

Before he could even think of ducking away, she turned her head in the direction from which the birds had come…

And she saw him.

Even from forty feet away her gasp was more than audible.

She immediately closed her legs, brought her hands over her breasts, and rose to her knees.

"I…I'm so, so sorry, Mary Lynn," he said, barely loud enough for her to have heard him over the roar of the surf. "Please, forgive me. I didn't know anyone was here." He started to turn away again.

Her voice stopped him. "Actually, it's okay, Doc. Really...please don't leave."

And, as quickly as she'd covered herself, she allowed her hands to fall away from her spellbinding breasts. He couldn't take his eyes from them as she knelt in the sand before him. Before he knew what was happening, he found himself taking three steps toward her.

He was now only thirty feet away.

"It's okay," she reiterated. The wind was blowing the ends of her hair about like the smoke from a genie's lamp. It moved provocatively, dancing this way and that. "Besides...I...well, you've already seen me anyway."

He hesitated. Was this really happening? He tried a few more steps.

Twenty feet.

Just then, he caught sight of her clothes draped over the bushes off to his right.

"I was attacked by a giant wave and I was letting them dry," she explained needlessly.

He nodded, never taking his eyes from her. "Would you like me to get them for you?"

She shrugged, then glanced down at her bare breasts. "Yes, I suppose that would be good. Thank you."

He walked over and hesitantly drew her dress, bra, and panties from the bush, then brought them to her on feet that could barely move and with knees that seemed almost unable to support his weight.

Ten feet.

He paused, then took the last few steps with his eyes now forced away from her and held them out to her, lowering his knapsack onto the sand at the same time.

"Thank you," she repeated softly as she took them from him. And when he turned toward her once again he saw that she was smiling faintly, shyly, at him with one of his favorite smiles. She showed no teeth, simply curled her stunning lips into a shape which, he was sure, could stop just about any man in his tracks. And that certainly included him.

She sat her clothes on her lap but made no move to put them on or cover herself further. "Actually, they're still damp," she explained. "If I put them on now, I'll probably start to shiver again."

He smiled in acknowledgement.

A few more waves came crashing in upon the sand.

"Please don't go," she repeated, perhaps in deference to his unbelieving ears. "Stay here with me…at least for a little while. Okay?"

And lo and behold, his mouth actually worked for a change.

"Yes, of course, Mary Lynn. I'd like that." The calm in his voice surprised him and seemed to do the same to her. He sat down beside her, then forced himself to look out at the ocean, even as he sensed her eyes upon him. But after scarcely a half-minute, he realized that there was apparently no reason to look away. She was the one who had invited him over here, after all. She obviously had no problem with him seeing her. Otherwise, she would at least have held her dress in front of or over herself in some manner or another.

After swallowing hard a couple of times, he turned toward her and looked straight into her eyes. She returned the look. Good heavens, her eyes were beautiful. They were the kind of brown that betrayed her wisdom as well as her good heart. Set beneath lush lashes that moved in slow, trusting blinks, they held his gaze fast.

More waves crashed to shore. Then:

"Mary Lynn, can I ask you why you're..."

"Why I'm here...doing what I was just doing? Or, why I invited you over?"

He smiled faintly. "Both, I suppose."

She smiled back. "Well, that's good because both questions have the same answer: You."

His heart leaped. "Pardon?"

"Yes, Doc...*you*." Her voice was ever soft and soothing as she went on. "You see, while I was lying on the sand, waiting for my clothes to dry, I started thinking about yesterday, when you were cutting those vines off me and you had your hands on me. I know it sounds strange, considering how frightened I'd been, but your touch just mesmerized me. I can't explain it, it just felt very, very good. Then..." She looked out at the waves for a moment. "I started thinking about you and Gina, which I admit I've been doing ever since I heard the two of you last night, and I couldn't stop imagining it—you...with her, I mean. Then, after a little while, I...started putting myself into the scene...you know...in place of Gina. I just couldn't stop picturing the two of us together. And then, after a few minutes..." She shrugged. "Well, I guess it got the better of me."

The Doc simply stared. He had no words.

She shrugged again. "Like I said, I couldn't stop. I just kept imagining that you were kissing *me*, touching *me*, and doing all the things to *me* that I'd imagined you doing to Gina." She looked him straight in the eye. "I don't like to think of myself as the jealous type, but, well, I guess in this case I am."

At that instant, the thrust of the surf became silent in the Doc's ears. His mind was in a whirl as he fought to process all this. Was he hearing her correctly?

There was a long silence as Mary Lynn looked at him, then down at her beautiful body, then back at him as he simply stared off into the waves —

thinking, his mind in complete and utter awe.

"Doc?"

He blinked back to reality. "Hm?"

"Is this making any sense?"

Another pause.

"I...I'm not sure." Another wave. "Perhaps."

She sighed. "I like Gina. I really do. I love her, really. We get along great together. She's always telling me about this man or that man...this romance or that. And I enjoy listening to her, um, lusty stories. But sometimes..." She shrugged. "Sometimes I can't help feeling that *I* would like to be the one who 'gets the man' for a change. Just once..."

Now it was she who paused. Many more waves came in. Then:

"I have feelings for you, Doc. I have for quite a while, actually. I've always admired you. I've always adored your handsome face. I've always been in awe of your amazing intellect. I've always cherished your sweet kindness..." She shrugged and smiled sheepishly. "And I've always noticed your...physique."

"Mary Lynn, I—"

She took a deep breath and turned her head toward the sea. "I guess what I'm trying to say is that—"

"Mary Lynn—"

"I want you."

He literally gasped at the words. "*You...* want *me*?"

She nodded slowly. "Like I've never wanted anyone before." Then, her voice now growing darker: "I want you, but I know that Gina wants you, too. She told me so, in fact. And any man would be crazy not to want to be with a movie star, especially a gorgeous, well-built, sexy movie star like Gina LaPlante."

She took a deep breath. "So, that's my confession."

Without thinking better of it, the Doc replied, "That's your *confession*?" He smiled warmly at her. "Mary Lynn, I'm no expert at relationships, to the say the least, but I'm quite certain that saying you are attracted to someone is *not* a 'confession.' It is anything *but* a confession. Indeed, it's an affirmation." He tilted his head disarmingly. "However, if you want to hear a confession, well, I believe I have a doozy of a confession to share with *you*, okay?"

Mary Lynn tilted her head quizzically, then nodded.

He leaned over, reached into his knapsack, and drew out his journal. As he began flipping pages he spoke. "I use part of this journal to record my scientific musings, observations, and research that I've conducted on the various species of wildlife I've discovered here." He stopped on a page. "A short while ago, I began a very different form of research, you might say. You see, as a result of my becoming increasingly distracted by and preoccupied with the two beautiful young women with whom I share this island, I decided that I might as well put my scientist's training to use and study you in earnest — study the two of you and try to answer the question I'd grown consumed by and which I am certain would have arisen in the mind of any man fortunate enough to be marooned here with both of you." He released a quiet self-incriminating laugh. "It's a very simple question, really: Which of you two women would a man most want to be with? That man, in this case, being me."

He paused to take in her mildly shocked expression. "So..." He swallowed. "I began taking notes on your beauty — on yours and Gina's — on your faces and figures, as well as — I'm sorry to admit this — the sexual attractiveness of your bodies."

Mary Lynn's expression suddenly darkened and she looked down. "Oh. Well, I guess that study didn't take very long, did it?" She laughed ruefully. "Mary Lynn Saunders...versus Hollywood movie star Gina LaPlante. Piece of cake."

"That's right, Mary Lynn. It wasn't very difficult. Here..." He flipped some pages. "Let me read you part of my last entry." He cleared his throat. "'And so, yes, I've elected to abandon this study for a multitude of reasons. First, because it was wrong. It was simply wrong to start looking upon two women, women who I respect, care for, and admire, and to study them with such carnal intentions. It was wrong for me to be comparing and contrasting such wonderful and good-hearted women in such a manner. Second, after having had a sexual encounter with Gina, it is most pointless to continue my study, as I will never have, or could ever have, the opportunity for a comparable experience with Mary Lynn. Third, because, I have already reached the end of this research by concluding that Mary Lynn is, in fact, the superior woman in matters of physical beauty and allure. Furthermore, she is unquestionably the woman with whom I would want most to —'"

"Doc!" Mary Lynn stared at him in shock. "You're crazy! You're choosing *me*? Against *Gina*?"

He smiled again and continued to read. "'I cite the following as the basis of my conclusion: First, Mary Lynn clearly possesses the most beautiful face. Certainly, Gina is an indescribably beautiful woman. Her fame alone would attest to that. But Mary Lynn's beauty is of an entirely different order. While Gina can boast beautiful lines, coloring, and facial features, as well as lovely hair, I feel that a part of her allure is due to the manner in which she presents herself as a sexual being. Men see the wantonness of her expression and the sexual hunger she proclaims with every move and this is very appealing to them, I'm quite sure.

"'Mary Lynn, on the other hand, possesses true beauty. Beauty that is real. Natural beauty that needs neither adornment nor fanfare. Beauty that manifests in her perfect lines, beautiful eyes, lovely hair, and enticing lips. I am crazy for her gorgeous mouth. Likewise, I would happily kiss those cheeks and those lips all day long.'"

He paused to take in Mary Lynn's ever widening open mouth. Then he continued to read.

"'Then there is the matter of their figures. Certainly, Gina's very full breasts and stunning hips are maddeningly attractive. But, once again, I must point out that a certain measure of her body's allure stems from the manner in which she flaunts it. She always dresses it so as to advertise and accentuate her assets. More often than not, she presents it and moves it in such a way that her curves are more than sufficiently showcased. Mary Lynn, on the other hand, has the more beautiful shape. It is not over-powering, but instead, beautifully proportioned, very firm and curvaceous in appearance, and it is simply more sexually attractive. It is just lovely. Exquisitely lovely. I will go so far as to regard it as resplendent. Furthermore, it matters not in the least what she wears or how she moves. The view is overwhelming beyond description and it is so from all directions, whether she makes any attempt to accentuate it or not.

"'All in all, in matters of the physical, Mary Lynn comes out on top with a face that is sweet yet seductive and a shape that is tantalizing beyond my ability to express. Add to that the energy she gives off—that warm, wonderful, and womanly energy. That mesmerizing charm and captivating goodness. Add to that her caring nature, her intuitive capabilities, her empathy, her sense of right and wrong, her work ethic, and her wisdom. Add in as well her sweet voice, her utterly captivating walk, and her beguiling facial expressions.

"'Result: Mary Lynn is, in fact, the woman for me and she is so by leaps and bounds. And so, after very careful and thorough consideration, I deem this research project closed and my mission accomplished. No further research is needed or is to be conducted.'"

By now, Mary Lynn was staring absently out at the sea. He reached out to touch her bare shoulder, mesmerized by its soft smoothness. Then he brought his fingers beneath her chin and turned her gently toward him. "Have I made myself clear?"

"Oh, you most certainly have, Doc," she replied, her gorgeous smile returning. "But I must say that, for all your intelligence, your essay contains one glaring error: the part about never having the opportunity for 'a comparable encounter with Mary Lynn.'"

She took a deep breath. "Frankly, I would give anything for such an encounter."

The Doc continued to look into her eyes, still not quite believing that it was he who was sitting on this beautiful beach next to this beautiful woman and having this particular conversation. He looked out at the sea, then back at her, back at the sea, back at her. Then he swallowed, finding the courage to respond: "Needless to say, I as well."

Barely one more wave made it to shore before he took her face in his hands and drank in the sight for a good long while, fighting as hard as he ever fought in order to force his next words past his lips. Finally, they came:

"Mary Lynn...may I kiss you?"

She nodded. "I think I've been wishing for that since Honolulu."

The instant his lips met hers, he knew. The exact moment when he claimed her mouth with his, he knew. This moment was and would continue to be of a whole other order than that which he'd shared with Gina. Holding her in his arms now — her beautiful, unclothed body — he was already aroused beyond imagination. He was keenly aware of the cool softness of her skin in every place where their bodies touched: her breasts, her hips, her thighs. Yes, it made him hungry. It made him hard. But it also made him happy. Happy, thrilled, and complete. Mary Lynn was the woman with the power to make him into the man he'd always been but was too caught up in a life over-filled with study, research, and academia to realize it.

Her mouth was sweet, he realized, as their tongues swirled slowly and gently across each other's. Sweet and velvety. But as he felt her tongue against his and her hand that was now touching his face, and her body that continued to press more and more snugly against him, he began to notice something even more captivating: Everything Mary Lynn did, every move she made, was infused with the same innocence and purity that she displayed every single day and with which she lived her life. And, as he was now discovering, this innocence appeared to have the power to entice him more deeply and completely than anything he could ever have imagined. Mary Lynn's innocence was, intriguingly, at the center of her power to allure. Coupled with her incredible beauty, it was the one-two punch that made her, he was certain, the most beautiful and sexually stimulating woman on earth.

A moment later, Mary Lynn gently pulled her lips from his and placed both her hands upon his shoulders. Slowly, they came together in the center and then proceeded to unbutton each button on his shirt, her eyes never leaving her hands. After she was finished, she pulled it off him in a single steady movement.

"Oh, Doc..." she breathed as she placed her palms against his chest, swallowing hard and shaking her head ever so slightly. "Oh, my..."

He simply moaned his reply as his own awestruck hands began to explore Mary Lynn's body. Goodness, everywhere he touched was soft, toned, smooth, and sweet—so indescribably sweet. His feelings of arousal multiplied to a level he had never known before. He gently cupped and stroked her breasts—so pretty and firm they were—and she threw her head back toward the intensely blue sky. God, he couldn't get enough of them! Each mound fit within his hand and he loved the feeling of her softly-pink nipples growing hard within his grasp. He pinched one delicately and Mary Lynn cooed her arousal.

The Doc removed the rest of his clothes. And then this sweet, innocent farmgirl did the last thing he would have expected. Gently but firmly, she pushed him from his kneeling position backward, forcing him to sit on his butt, legs outstretched. Then she walked on her knees to him and eased herself down upon his thighs, her artfully rounded hip pressing deeply against his stomach. The Doc's mouth opened as wide as his eyes. She shifted herself, making the two of them quite comfortable, met his chest with hers, then filled his mouth with her tongue.

As they kissed away a bit of their pent-up longing, he continued to explore her body with his hands. It struck him as scientifically impossible that her curves could feel so soft and yet so firm at the same time. But, impossible or not, it was just so and, after a few moments, he decided to file this imponderable away for the moment and enjoy...just enjoy...and marvel himself silly.

Their breaths quickened accordingly.

And all the while, as he looked out over her shoulder at the ocean once again, he tried and tried again to grasp the fact that, yes, he was holding and kissing Mary Lynn Saunders on this beach and getting to know her in this most intimate way. Mary Lynn Saunders, the most beautiful, sweet, alluring, and remarkable woman he'd ever known...with him!

As smart a man as he was, the Doc was certain that he would never come to understand how such a miracle could ever have come to be.

CHAPTER ELEVEN

Finnegan and the Captain huffed their way from the lagoon to the clearing, each holding a handle from a large bamboo basket filled to the brim with lobsters. By the time they set it down on the dining table, the Captain was breathless.

"Best batch ever," he said proudly between pants.

Finnegan grinned and nodded. "They sure are, Cap. I can't wait for dinner."

Just then the Powells emerged from their hut, Mrs. Powell looking ravishing in her lime green silk dress, matching plumed hat, and diamonds galore, Mr. Powell, in his dashing cream summer suit and hat that always made him look like a would-be plantation owner.

As they walked over to the table, Mr. Powell said, "Well, gentlemen, anything good in there?" He peered inside and chuckled. "By George, I must say, there certainly is!"

Mrs. Powell looked in as well and nodded her approval. "Yes, well, do be darlings and see to it that Mary Lynn sets aside the very best ones for the Powells."

Everyone laughed good-naturedly as the Powells went over to their chaise lounges in front of their hut to sit.

The Captain leaned over and murmured into Finnegan's ear: "Just between you and me, I say the *best* lobsters should go to the ones who caught them and lugged them up here."

"I second that, Cap!" Finnegan replied as the two began placing the twelve lobsters into a tub of water next to the table. "And I have dibs on those two babies right there."

A moment later, as they continued to work, the Captain looked around to see if they were alone. Then he looked up at Finnegan and shook his head ruefully.

Finnegan noticed. "Still thinking about it, huh?"

The Captain nodded, scowling. "I still can't believe it—Gina and the Doc going hog-wild like that last night. The whole thing has been bugging me ever since."

"You and me both. I can't believe the Doc getting so lucky! It's bad enough he got to feel her up. Now *this*." Finnegan shook his head ruefully as well. "It just ain't fair, Cap. I mean, the Doc doesn't even like girls!"

The Captain sighed. "Apparently, he does now, little buddy."

Finnegan shrugged it aside. "Maybe not. I mean, maybe Gina seduced *him*."

The Captain considered that for a second. "Maybe, but either way you're right...that Doc of ours is one lucky son of a bitch."

"That's for sure. I mean, all I can think about is him climbing on top of Gina and—"

The Captain held up his hand to cut him off. "All right, that's enough, Finnegan. I know I brought it up, but it isn't going to do either of us any good to go on agonizing about all that for days on end. Come on now, we've got the best lobsters of the season right here. Let's keep our minds on that, okay?"

He then looked up and around the clearing. "Better tell Mary Lynn about these so she can start getting them cooked." He cupped his hand to his mouth. "Mary Lynn! Come out here and see what Finnegan and I caught for lunch!"

He waited. Silence.

"Mary Lynn?" he called again.

Gina came out of her hut with a watering can. "She's not here, Cap'n. I haven't seen her since breakfast, in fact."

"Maybe she went swimming," Finnegan offered.

Gina shook her head. "Both of her bathing suits are hanging on the line. Maybe the Doc knows where she is," she added with a telltale blush, then began watering the flowers in the boxes outside her window.

The Captain nodded. "Maybe. Well, thanks anyway, Gina." He cupped his hand to his mouth once more. "Hey, Doc!"

He waited again. More silence.

"Doc?"

The two sailors looked at each other. "Well, I guess he's out, too," the Captain said.

"Yeah, probably out studying tree frogs humping or something," Finnegan offered, grinning.

The Captain shook his head and frowned. "I don't know. It's not like them to just wander off without telling anyone."

Finnegan looked up at him. "Do you think we should look for them?"

"Yes, I do, in fact. I think we all should search for them, especially if anyone wants lobster for dinner." He placed the last one into the tub, then turned to Gina and the Powells. "Okay, listen up, everyone. It's not like either the Doc or Mary Lynn to go off without telling anyone. I'm sure they're both fine, but, just as a precaution, I suggest we all go out looking for them."

"Sure, I'll go," Gina offered.

The Captain smiled. "That's great. Gina. I appreciate your help. Why don't you head to the west end of the island first? Finnegan and I will cover the east end. Stay on the paths and don't stay out any longer than, say, a half-hour or so. Otherwise, we'll have to come looking for *you*, too!"

"Okay, Cap'n," she said and walked away, swinging her luscious ass wide as always.

Next, he turned to the Powells. "Now, if you two will—"

The Captain stopped in mid-sentence when he noticed that Mr. Powell was paying no attention to him whatsoever, his eyes fixed hard upon Gina's butt—really hard, in fact. A slow devious grin had worked its way onto his face.

Just then, Mrs. Powell caught him staring and her mouth couldn't have opened any wider. "Why, Preston! Whatever on earth are you doing, you…you lecher!"

Startled, Mr. Powell tore his gaze away. "But Sweetey, be reasonable! After all, any man in the world would have—"

"*You* are not *any man*! You are a Powell! And you are *my* husband!" She nodded decisively. "Therefore, I forbid any such indecent behavior from you from now on and that's final!"

"Mr. Powell—" the Captain began.

Now Mr. Powell's dander was on the rise as well. "Well! Perhaps there would be no such behavior from me a-tall if my wife were only to offer a little…shall we say—"

Mrs. Powell gasped and clutched her hands to her chest. "Preston Powell the Third! How *dare* you speak of such indelicacies in front of the Captain and Finnegan! I've a good mind to…to withhold my favors!"

"Mr. Powell—"

Mr. Powell laughed uproariously. "Withhold favors? Ha! You've been withholding them straight since 1953! Ha! Ha!"

Mrs. Powell looked ready to faint. "Why…why…the nerve! The gall!"

The Captain was growing exasperated. "As I was say—"

"Yes, of course, Captain, we'd be delighted to help," Mr. Powell piped up, obviously in an attempt to diffuse the situation.

"Well, thank you. I appreciate your interest." The Captain replied. Frankly, he was surprised that Mr. Powell would so readily offer to do anything that required expending energy.

"Yes, yes, of course. Now then, I hereby offer a $5,000 reward for the Doc's and Mary Lynn's safe return!" he announced as he began reaching into his back pocket for his wallet.

The Captain scowled. "Oh, brother! C'mon, Finnegan. Let's go." He took two paces, then pointed to their hut and said, "You'd better grab my binoculars. They're on my sea chest. We may need 'em."

"Sure, Cap." Finnegan went and retrieved the binoculars, then the two set off for the east end of the island amidst the resumption of the Powells' squabble.

* * * *

Twenty minutes later, Finnegan suddenly found himself with a boner the size of Lake Michigan.

"Holy shit, Cap! Holy ever-loving shit! I can't believe it!"

The two had just arrived at the top of a tree-covered hill overlooking the east beach. Finnegan had the binoculars trained upon the scene that was taking place on the sand below. He instinctively began rubbing his crotch.

The Captain looked at him, annoyed. "What are you — what is it *now*, Finnegan?"

Finnegan simply kept on peering and rubbing and shaking his head slowly. "I can't believe it," he repeated more softly. "She's even better naked!" Next, he let out a low whistle. "And would you look at that ass?"

"Can't believe what? Who's naked? Whose ass? Here, let me see those." The Captain pried the binoculars from Finnegan's hands.

"Mary Lynn! Look, Cap, look! She's with the Doc! And that filthy bastard has his hands all over her—and she's ever-loving *naked*!" He slapped his leg. "That makes two gorgeous women in two days for that son of a bitch."

The Captain peered down at the beach for barely two seconds. Then a peculiar look came over him and he lowered the binoculars from his eyes.

Finnegan stared. "What are you doing? Don't you want to see 'em?"

The Captain's look turned sober and he shook his head. "No, little buddy. I *don't* want to see them. And neither do you. And that's an order!"

Finnegan stared again. "*What?* What are you—"

"Listen, Finnegan, I know you and I are just a couple of horny and hard-up sailors, but..." He smiled sadly. "It's one thing to peep at Gina, you know? I mean, it's more than obvious that she *wants* men to peep at her, right? But, come on, that's Mary Lynn down there, for goodness' sake—and I do mean *goodness*. I know we ogle her and think indecent things about her sometimes, but I just don't feel right about peeping at her like this. It's wrong. Now, if it were anyone else—with a body like hers— sure, I'd be looking all day and I'd probably be hard as a mainsail mast the whole time, but..." He sighed. "We just can't. Not with our Mary Lynn."

Finnegan's winced in frustration, then lowered his head and sighed. "I guess you're right, Cap. Okay, fine, I won't look." He and the Captain turned back toward the path. Then his look brightened. "But I still get to call the Doc a lucky son of a mother-fucking bitch, right?"

The Captain laughed. "You and me both. Come on, let's head back to camp. Looks like we're going to have to cook those lobsters ourselves this time."

* * * *

As Gina walked along the path that led to the island's west beach, her mind was in a tizzy over the previous night. What, in the name of Richard Burton, had gone wrong? What had she done to cause the Doc to lose interest in having sex — with inarguably one of the sexiest women on earth?

Arriving at the end of the path, she stepped out onto the sand and scanned the beach from one end to the other. She saw nothing but sand, sun, and surf.

But as she continued to look it suddenly dawned on her that Mary Lynn almost never used this beach anyway, unless everyone was here for a luau or something. She rolled her eyes — coming out here had been a complete waste of her time. Mary Lynn almost always used the small beach on the east end. That had to be where she was.

As for the Doc? She smiled wryly. Probably out searching for his stupid birds.

She scanned the wide beach one more time, just to be sure. A second later, she turned and started backtracking to the place that Mary Lynn often referred to as her 'sanctuary.'

Along the way, she started thinking about the Doc again. Last night everything had started out so wonderfully. He was more than turned-on and she was more than ready, willing, and able to take him to the moon and back. But then, as soon as he started actually having sex with her, he acted like it was no big deal to him. It made no sense, no sense whatsoever.

She shook her head sadly. This sort of thing had never happened to her before—not to Gina LaPlante. Maybe he was just overwhelmed by the experience of losing his virginity. Or, maybe, despite his recent bout of horniness, the sex bug just wasn't inside him.

Well, whatever it was, it certainly wasn't her fault! If she couldn't turn him on, nobody could!

That was when she started to make out the faint sounds of voices just ahead.

The path she'd been walking on ended abruptly and Gina found herself looking out over a scene that brought her jaw to the ground.

She crouched down behind a rock to avoid being seen, then looked again.

There, not ten yards away, were the Doc...and Mary Lynn! They were completely nude and lying on the sand cuddling one another! They were lying on their sides, the Doc behind her. He was gently stroking her hip. And she was gently cooing in delight. Next, he drew his fingers through her hair oh-so-tenderly. Then she turned her face back toward him and they shared a soft, lingering kiss. It was a truly beautiful scene and oh-so romantic...

It was all Gina could do to keep from throwing up.

She wanted nothing more than to turn and get the hell out of here as quickly as she could. But her curiosity got the better of her and, instead, she cupped her ear and listened in.

Though their voices were diffused by the sound of the waves, she could still hear plenty.

"This...*this* is what I always wanted..." he said, smiling dreamily.

"Mmm...me, too," she said, smiling dreamily in return.

Then:

"Did you enjoy being with Gina?" she asked.

"Yes. Yes, in truth, I did," he replied. "Gina is a very beautiful and sexually enticing woman. Any man would be crazy not to fall for her."

"I see," she said. "So, that makes you…"

"Certifiably, inarguably crazy…for you."

Another kiss…more cooing…and more cuddling…

Gina's blood was just about ready to boil. She'd had it. Casting one more furious look toward the beach, she stood, spun around on her heels, and hurried back to the clearing.

As she stormed through the jungle, she simply could not let go of the single thought:

How *dare* he! How dare he turn up his nose at Gina LaPlante!

* * * *

Finnegan and the Captain had just made it back to the clearing when Gina marched up behind them.

"Gina! There you are!" the Captain said with a grin — a grin that fell immediately when he realized that she looked about ready to explode — or cry. "Oh, my goodness, what's wrong?"

Gina was so upset she could barely speak. In fact, she was nearly hysterical. "I'll tell you what's wrong!" she wailed. "Apparently, Mr. Man of Science can't put two and two together and realize that *no* man says no to Gina LaPlante!"

She started to cry. The Captain took her in his arms. "There, there, Gina. Finnegan and I saw everything, too."

"Yeah, we saw everything," Finnegan echoed. "Boy, the Doc sure had his hands full, didn't he?"

Gina cried harder.

"Finnegan!"

Finnegan hung his head. "Sorry, Cap'n. Sorry, Gina."

"Gina, it's okay," the Captain went on soothingly. "Please don't cry. You're a *very* beautiful woman. Why, you're the most beautiful and sexy woman we've ever seen!"

Gina looked up, sniffling. "Even better than Mary Lynn?"

The Captain's mouth opened and closed. "Well, I...I guess I wouldn't *really* know for sure about that. I mean, we haven't exactly —"

Gina's eyes opened wide. "You wouldn't know? You wouldn't *know*? After that show I gave the two of you at the waterfall the other day? And you still *'wouldn't know'*?"

Both men winced at her words.

"Gee, Gina, I'm really sorry about that," Finnegan began. "We didn't mean to look — well, okay, I guess we kinda did. What I mean is, we didn't mean to get off on it the way we did — well, I mean —"

"Finnegan!"

Gina seemed not to have heard. She glanced down at her incredible body, poorly hidden inside her glittering peach evening dress. "So...you wouldn't know...?"

Without another word, Gina reached back and unzipped it. Then she pushed both straps from her shoulders. The dress fell to the ground in a gorgeous peachy puddle.

Finnegan's and the Captain's jaws followed suit.

"Holy Moby Dick!" the Captain breathed.

"Um, I think you dropped something," Finnegan replied, licking his upper lip.

"So, you wouldn't know," she repeated as she reached back and unfastened her flame-red bra, pulled it off, and dropped it to the ground. "You wouldn't know *who's* better?" She moved the fingers of both hands across her mango-sized mammaries tauntingly. "What could the Doc have possibly found wrong with these? Aren't they...nice enough?"

"Sweet Jesus!" Finnegan breathed, leaning forward, his eyes all but leaping from their sockets.

"Well, I...I...I..." the Captain began, unable to go on.

"They're sure nice enough for us, Gina!" Finnegan enthused, nodding emphatically and drooling out of both sides of his mouth.

"And what about these nipples?" She dragged her fingertips across their pinkish-brown goodness. "Do they at least meet *your* male standards?"

"Mother of King Neptune, yes!" the Captain reassured her.

Finnegan just kept nodding like a wind-up toy.

Now Gina was hooking her thumbs inside the waistband of her matching panties – panties that fit her form so precisely that nothing whatsoever was left to the imagination. Seconds later, she pulled them down, down, down, over her never-ending thighs, to the ground, then stepped out of them. When she was finished, she crossed one leg in front of the other, struck a mouth-watering pinup girl pose, smiled seductively, and waited.

"Sweet ever-fucking-loving Jesus," Finnegan murmured. "Look at her, Cap. Look at her!"

"I...I...I...I'm looking, Finnegan. I'm looking."

"Aren't I curvy enough for *him*?" Gina asked, pouting, as she ran her hands from her thighs, around her hips, past her breasts, then straight up over her head.

"You're sure as hell curvy enough for *us*," Finnegan replied. "Ain't she, Cap?"

"I...I...I...yes, Finnegan, of course, she is. Now, would you shut up and let the woman continue?"

"And my bush..." She lowered her arms and trailed her fingers through her flaming triangle.

"What man wouldn't want to get lost in *this*?"

"Not us, Gina!" the Captain assured her, licking his lips.

"No, sir, not us!" Finnegan concurred. "But the Doc? Well…"

To which the Captain whipped off his hat, whacked Finnegan on the top of his head, then put it back on.

"Sorry, Gina," Finnegan mumbled.

"Well, what about my ass…?" She pirouetted slowly and caressed her exquisite cheeks for them. "Isn't it at least *almost* as nice as Mary Lynn's?"

"God, yes!" the Captain and Finnegan answered in unison.

Gina turned back and dropped her eyes toward the straining bulges in each seaman's pants.

"Well, well, it looks like your two little shipmates want to come out and play, too," she commented dryly. "Why don't you let them out for a breath of fresh air?"

Both men looked from side to side with giddy, nervous grins.

"Right here?" Finnegan squeaked.

"Where the Powells might see?" the Captain asked, swallowing hard.

Gina smiled saucily and shook her head. Then she crooked her finger at them, turned, and began wiggling her way into the jungle.

Finnegan and the Captain exchanged almost delirious grins as they followed close behind her, keeping a hand in their pants and their eyes utterly glued to Gina's swaying, canting, flexing, meaty, and oh-so-gorgeous Ginaness.

CHAPTER TWELVE

Mr. Powell had just come out of his hut with his bamboo golf clubs in hand. He'd had plans to do some putting, but now stood, frozen, just outside the door, on the verge of fainting.

He'd seen everything.

The clubs clattered to the ground and his silk-clad member lurched, very ungentlemanly-like at the sight of Gina's strip show and her bare-bottomed exit from the clearing. He craned his neck until she and her two followers were out of sight. Then he sat down hard on his chaise, wiping perspiration from his brow.

Within seconds his trademark "Wolf of Wall Street" grin spread deviously across his face.

"I wonder how much she'd charge to do that for *me*?" he wondered aloud.

Just then, the grin fell from his face when he realized that Mrs. Powell had come out of the hut and was standing directly behind him, seething up a storm.

"Preston Powell the Third! What on earth are you doing?"

"Never mind that, Sweetey," he replied, unable to stop his grin from reappearing. "What in thunder do you suppose *they're* doing?"

* * * *

Finnegan and the Captain continued to follow Gina through the jungle, their eyes still glued to her spellbinding nudity.

"So, I guess we're the consolation prizes, huh?" the Captain said as they approached the waterfall.

Gina stopped and turned to them, smiling wickedly. "Well, why don't you fellas get into your birthday suits like I did and we'll find out."

The Captain grinned nervously as he reached for his belt.

Finnegan grinned deviously as he began to unzip his sailor pants.

Little did she know…

Feast your eyes and hold onto your hat, darling…

Then:

"Oh…oh…oh, my *god!*"

Gina's gasp and stunned expression were so comically incredulous that even Finnegan and the Captain had to laugh. Her face was scrunched, her jaw had come practically unhinged, and her eyes were in utter shock. "Finnegan! Y-you…you…"

"Surprise, surprise," Finnegan said dryly.

"Yeah, surprise, surprise," the Captain echoed, glancing over at his massively-endowed shipmate with a look that was one part envy and two parts pride-by-association.

"I…I had no idea! Finnegan! For god's sake, you're a Clydesdale! You're…huge! And, oh, it's *so* gorgeous!" Gina shook her head back and forth, still staring. "Three years on this island together and you think you know someone…"

"My pride and joy," Finnegan said, matter-of-fact, proudly hefting his eleven-incher. Gina's reaction was no surprise; he'd been shocking and scaring the hell out of chicks since he was sixteen.

"It's…astounding," Gina agreed. Then, turning to the Captain, she took in the sight of his endowment and nodded her approval. "And *you've* certainly been well-blessed there, too, Cap'n."

The Captain smiled sheepishly. "Well, I'm no Finnegan, that's for sure, but it gets me where I need to go. Besides, I don't think Finnegan or I can take *all* the credit in this case, Gina." He chuckled. "I mean, after spending the past five minutes walking behind that absolutely stunning backside of yours…" He looked down at his swollen member and chuckled. "Well, this sort of thing was bound to happen!"

Gina smiled. "So, you boys enjoyed our little stroll, did you?"

"Enjoyed it?" Finnegan looked at her in disbelief, then shook his head. "Uh, no, Gina. I *enjoy* fishing. I *enjoy* eating lobster. I *enjoy* whittling. But feasting my eyes on that ass of yours? No, I'd say that goes *way* beyond 'enjoyed,' eh, Cap?"

"He's absolutely right, Gina. I mean, *we* had no idea either!"

"Yeah," Finnegan piped up. "Three years on this island together and you think you know someone…"

Pouting once again, Gina ran her hands tauntingly across her cheeks. "Well, why wasn't it nice enough for *him*, then?"

"Who cares? The Doc's a fucking idiot." Finnegan replied, brushing it aside. "Besides, it's *way* nice enough for us!"

"By a mile, Gina!" the Captain amended, nodding emphatically.

Finnegan looked over at him and gave a short laugh. The Captain sure looked stupid standing there with his dick sticking straight out, wearing nothing but his captain's hat. Then, realizing that he must look pretty stupid, too, with his own sailor hat still on, he quickly yanked it off and threw it to the ground.

The Captain saw him and did the same.

"Well," Gina went on. "I'm glad *someone* on this island appreciates my assets." She turned sideways to give them another view. "But why are you acting so surprised? You boys had plenty of time to check out all my goodies those few times you had those binoculars on me."

The Captain nodded. "True, but this is a whole different situation. Binoculars or not, seeing your gorgeous tush from three feet away is a whole different thing altogether."

"Yeah, it's a whole different thing," Finnegan echoed. "It's so close now we could practically reach out and touch it."

Gina turned again and bent forward tauntingly. "Then why don't you go right ahead!"

In a split second, Finnegan and the Captain stepped forward and each took one of her soft, supple cheeks in their hands.

Then, amidst nonstop, overlapping moans, the two horny sailors began rubbing, caressing, and gently squeezing Gina LaPlante's beauteous backside.

Gina began giggling and cooing. "Mmm, nice, isn't it, boys?"

"I can't believe it," Finnegan whispered as if to himself. "After three years of ogling and fantasizing, we actually have our hands on this thing. Man-o-man!" He moved his hand to the deepest part of her cheek and gave it one long deep but gentle squeeze. He was beside himself with delight.

Gina's ass is in my hands.

Gina's gorgeous ass is in my hands.

Gina's hot, gorgeous, and very naked ass is in my hands!

Moments later:

"Oh, boys..." Gina said tauntingly, "my bottom sure does feel grateful for all that undivided attention. But don't forget that there's a lot more of me to explore."

"In a minute," Finnegan replied, still groping away. "You've been wiggling and swinging this thing in front of us every chance you got for the past three years! After torturing us for all that time, you don't think I'm letting go of it *that* soon, do you?"

"He's got a point, there, Gina," the Captain pointed out.

"I'm more interested in the point he's got down *there!*" Gina countered, looking back over her shoulder and nodding toward Finnegan's case-in-point.

"Well," the Captain countered, "we're more interested in what you've got pointing at *us*," the Captain said.

"Point well taken," Gina replied and thrust her ass back a little further.

And so, the happy exploration of Gina's gluteal goodies continued.

But after another minute or two, Finnegan did begin to feel the call from her more northern latitudes. Finally, he let go, then reached around her with both hands and began the same process with her free-hanging breasts. Yes, seeing them through binoculars was one thing, but this — he pressed into the incredibly soft undersides, then squeezed them full-on — this was pleasure of a whole other order.

Yes siree, this was better than any rescue would ever have been! He was now convinced that bungling all those rescue operations really was turning out to be the smartest thing he ever did!

"Hey, Finnegan! Let me in there, too!" the Captain ordered as the three horny castaways continued with the feel-up frenzy of all time.

A moment later, Gina stood, turned back around, looked down at their twin stiff masts, smiled, and said, "Well, now, I would say you're quite primed! And, no, given your, shall I say, male blessings, this is most certainly *not* a consolation prize. I intend to enjoy myself very, very thoroughly …as I'm sure you will as well."

The two men stared. "You mean you want us both? Right here? Right now?" the Captain asked in utter disbelief.

"Both. Right here. Right now," Gina replied without a trace of a smile, her eyes still drinking in the sight of their now-public privates.

As Finnegan and the Captain stared in amazement, Gina simply turned and walked just a few steps to where a lush bedding of moss lay.

"Who wants to be first?" she asked, tilting her head coyly.

"I do, I do!" Finnegan offered, raising his hand and grinning.

"Now wait just a minute! Who's Captain around here?"

"He does, he does," Finnegan amended, his grin now gone.

"Cap'n it is," Gina declared. "And my woman's intuition tells me that you're a doggy-style sort of a guy. Without another word, she got down on all fours and thrust her wide-flaring lady-goodies at them. "Ahoy, there, Captain," she taunted. "Give it to me. Give it to me good." She opened her legs wider. "And don't worry, I'm already slippery as buttered lobster down there, so you're good to go."

By way of a reply, the Captain simply knelt down, positioned himself right up against her supple protrusions, then slipped right inside her pussy in a single, swift motion.

"*Ahhhhhhhhh!*" he breathed.

"*Mmmmmmmm!*" Gina replied.

Finnegan simply stood there, enjoying the view immensely. There was Gina, burying her shoulders into the moss and moving in lock-step with the Captain as he thrust in and out, panting and gasping like crazy.

He let out a low whistle. Hot damn, she looked good. Gina didn't just have a great body, she knew exactly how to use it too!

Then he glanced over at the Captain. As always, he was pumping way too fast for a man of his very limited sexual stamina—especially while doing it with a gorgeous master sexpert like Gina. He smiled a faint, knowing smile and nodded. It was just a matter of time—seconds, really…

Yup. Barely a minute after he'd begun, the Captain threw his head back toward the sky. "I'm coming, Gina," he murmured, breathless, his body beginning to shudder. "Oh god, oh god, oh god, I'm coming…I'm coming…I can't help it…it just feels so, so good! I'm—oh—oh…*oh, no!*"

Finnegan doubled over in a fit of laughter. He'd known all along about the Captain's penchant for brevity ever since the time they shared the same hooker on Waikiki five years ago. He'd been so quick that night, he should have been granted a partial refund.

"Don't you dare stop!" Gina ordered him, still pumping. "I don't care that you came already. I want you to keep fucking me!"

"But…but Gina," the Captain replied, still gasping, "I just c-can't keep going. I just can't keep…" And that was it. Without another word or another stroke, he simply fell backward in a heap onto the moss, staring up at the sky, dazed and spent.

Gina stood and turned around, hands on hips, and stared down at the Captain with a mock scolding glare. "That's it? That's all you can give me?"

"For...now..." he replied, panting away. "I'm just so...tired. And you were just so...so... incredible."

Finnegan shook his head, forced down his grin, and strolled right up to Gina. "Don't worry, darlin'. I'll handle this now," he said with an air of cockiness and authority.

Then, before she could say a word, he pulled her into his arms and brought his lips to hers.

Holy God, where had this woman been all his life — or at least for the past three years, he wondered as he coaxed her tongue deep into her mouth. At the same time, he brought his hands behind her, boldly claiming the mounds of her full-figured butt, and held her tight against him, feeling her soft, curvy goodness right up flush against his hardness.

His cock thrust straight out, straight between her legs and out the other side as he sucked her tongue and then allowed her to return the gesture. He loved the way her cheeks pulled in tight as she sucked him inside her luscious mouth. His tongue wrestled with hers until he could barely stand it any longer.

"That's one hell of a set of lips you have there, Gina," he said between kisses.

"And those aren't the only ones," she replied, stepping back and nodding down at her pussy. "I've got another set all ready for you…anytime you're ready."

"Good to hear, Gina. And I see you rolled out the red carpet, too."

Gina drew her fingers playfully through her bush. "Only the best for my well-hung guests," she said, still eyeing his love-handle with undisguised awe.

That said, Finnegan simply eased her long, supple movie-star body back down onto the moss and flipped her over with all the grace of a short-order cook flipping burgers.

Gina immediately raised herself up onto her knees, then spread her legs for him. Finnegan grinned wickedly as he looked down at her, all vulnerable and wanton at the same time. Then…he simply waited.

And waited.

And waited some more.

It was a tried and true technique of his: Always make 'em wait. Always make the chick stew a little bit; take your sweet time and show her that you're in complete control — of her, of yourself, and of the situation. It never failed to help heat 'em up just a tad.

After several seconds, Gina looked back at him.

"Well?" she asked softly. "What are you waiting for?"

He looked down at her with just a trace of a confident smile as he knelt down behind her, his massive member pointed straight at her nicely trimmed and groomed pussy. "Just waiting for you to be a good girl and ask nicely."

Gina looked back at him with surprise, then shook her head in amazement. "Three years on this island and you think you know someone." Suddenly, grinning wickedly, she reached back and grabbed his cock. "Hm, how about I be a *bad* girl and ask naughty instead!" Before Finnegan could respond, she pulled him inside her. "Now...fuck me, sailin' man!"

"That's better," Finnegan replied. With that, he began stroking the depths of her goody bag with his usual zest and well-practiced skill.

Well-practiced except, of course, during the past three years. Like his dad always told him: Sex is like a game of cards...if you don't have a good partner, you'd better have a good hand. Luckily, as far as he was concerned, making love to a hot lady was like riding a bike. In seconds, it all came back to him and he soon found himself settling in to his well-admired stride.

"Holy god!" she cried out. "This is like a five-course dinner!"

"Oooh, yeah," he crooned.

Yeah, forget that tropical tart in Waikiki. Never mind the surfer chick on Maui. Who cares about the dozens of single female passengers over the years who didn't have the money for their three-hour outing aboard the Moray and who were invited on the tour anyway? All Finnegan could think at the moment was that Gina had every one of them beat hands down.

Hands down, shoulders down, and ass up, that is.

There really was no comparison, he realized as he slipped boldly and deeply into her love tunnel. Gina LaPlante was everything she made herself out to be. Yes, she truly was *the* sex goddess of all time. Between the beauty of her face, her thick and luxurious red hair—which, right now he was in the process of grabbing by the handful—the pillowy softness of her wide ass as he thrust against it with everything he had, and the almost magical velvety softness of her pussy, wrapped expertly and snugly around him, ho baby, it most certainly was a dream come true!

A dream that just kept on coming.

And the best part was that, unlike the Captain, he could go all night if he wanted to.

Yeah, he might not be the brightest sailor out there. Okay, he might have had more than his share of goof-ups. He might accidentally have stamped out signal fires and sunk rescue rafts. He might have fallen asleep while on sentry duty the time that Navy helicopter whizzed by. And there was no denying that it was he who'd accidentally dropped the lantern inside the men's latrine hut and sent the whole stinking thing up in flames. But if there was one thing—just one thing—he could pat himself on the back for, it was this: When it came to sex, nobody, but nobody, could hold on like him! Even while doing it with the sexiest chick on the planet, as he was doing right now, he could take her for as long a ride as he wanted and as long as she wanted and never, ever run out of gas.

Which was a very good thing because he sure didn't want this experience—the greatest thrill he ever had—to be over anytime soon. Not until he'd had a chance to savor all of Gina's earthy delights. After all, he still had plenty of curves to fondle and positions to try.

So, as the Captain looked on in abject envy and unbridled awe, Finnegan then took her on her back, her legs spread from Maui to Manilla, his tongue deep in her mouth the whole time. Then he had her on her side, spooning against her silky back and butt, gripping her tits like the handlebars of a motorcycle. Next, he had her standing spread eagle up against the wall of stone beneath the tiny waterfall, having the splash of his life, wishing like hell he had a bar of soap to use on her right then. Then he turned her around, backed her up against that wall, and went face-to-face, molesting-style. Finally, he had her bent completely over an enormous, moss-covered log, totally at his mercy, arms and legs stretched out wide, her ass pointing straight up at the dimming sky.

Three years, he started thinking at one point as he continued to thrust away. Three years on this island, watching this beauty strut her stuff all over the place from dawn to dusk. Three years of checking her out. Three years of hard-ons. Three years of wanting nothing more than to be doing...

Exactly what he was doing right now.

Three years of torture was finally being given its release. Three years of wondering and imagining what it might be like were now officially over.

Now he knew.

"Ooh, Finnegan...that's just...incredible," she acknowledged through gasping breaths. "It's just—it's just—"

"It sure is," he interjected, sliding his length all the way in, then all the way back out, then thrusting all the way back in again. He was amazed at how tight she felt, given her years of prior experience. Then again, like him, she had had three years of celibacy—three years to regain her taut tone—and now he was the one lucky enough to savor the gripping results. Savoring the feel of her flesh. Savoring the sight of her legendary body and gaping ass. Savoring the sounds of her moans and groans. Savoring the scents of both her perfume and her heat.

Savoring the heady rush of once again doing what he did best—making love to a hot, lusty woman and being in charge from start to finish.

Not that Gina didn't issue any commands of her own...

"Touch my clit," she ordered in a husky whisper. "Touch it all over the place. Come on, Finnegan—slow, fast, circles, squiggles, taps, tickles, write a love letter with your finger, I don't care...whatever makes you—and me—happy..."

"Sure thing, little lady," he replied. He quickly brought his right hand to her very excited little nub and did everything she asked for and more, his fingers moving faster and faster, their point of contact growing harder and harder. Meanwhile, his left hand amused itself in her long, luxurious red hair, bathing in it, swimming through it, and pulling handfuls of it back just hard enough to remind Gina who was boss.

"*Hoooo-weeeee!*" Gina screeched as she continued to match his every thrust with one of her own.

"I second that, Gina," he enthused. Greatest ride ever...and I've ridden plenty."

"Well, get ready, because yours truly is about to shift into high gear!"

"*Yeeooww!*" Finnegan called out, just as Gina began squeezing her pussy tight as a tourniquet around his shaft in a slow, sensuous rhythm that blew his mind. "What the—?"

Gina giggled. "Specialty of the house!"

"My compliments to the chef!" Finnegan called out, grinning like a jockey on the winning horse. Ooh, yeah, this—*this*—was the good stuff!

A little too good, actually, for, thanks to Gina's little maneuver, he quickly found himself moving involuntarily past the point of no return for just about the first time in his life. This was just...too...too good. There was just no way...no way he could maintain this any longer.

And so, after just a few more minutes, Finnegan had no choice but to speed up...and up...and up...moving at lightning speed now, stroking deep and hard until Gina's wildest squeals rang through the darkening jungle at least twice as loud as the night before, when she was with the Doc.

"Oh...oh...oh...Finnegan! Ooh...yes...yes... that's it! That's it! That's—that's just...incredible, baby! That's just...*oooooooh-weeeeeeeee!*"

"Oh, Gina," he grunted, very out of control and very un-Finnegan-like, as he began to come.

"Oh god...ho god...ho ho god...*Gi-i-i...na-a-ah!*" He slammed into her one final time, then collapsed on top of her, breathing hard, matching Gina's breathing, pant for pant.

"That..." he heard Gina say throatily, "was just..."

"Ooh, yes, it was," he finished for her, grinning wickedly. "And you're quite welcome."

Always his favorite parting line.

Seconds later, he climbed off of Gina, stood, and pulled her to her feet. After a lingering and very wet finishing-up kiss, they turned and saw the Captain still sitting on a rock off to one side, still naked, shaking his head in disbelief.

"Little buddy," he said, "you never cease to amaze me. How in the name of the Seven Seas do you—"

"Told you before, Cap...everybody's a captain at something. Even me!" He hooked his thumb toward Gina. "That is, me and this movie star over here."

"Ooh, you're so right, little—oops, I mean *big* buddy," Gina cooed, claiming his mouth with hers once again. "And, believe me, we are so very, very good at this!"

Then, with a foxy grin, she turned to the Captain. "As for you! I'd say it's high time you got in a little bit of advanced therapy, courtesy of the one and only Gina LaPlante. How about coming over here and I'll teach you the age-old art of taking your foot off the gas pedal and enjoying the scenic route for a change!"

* * * *

Meanwhile, on the Isle of Tiazanu...

King Palawani looked out over the darkened sea and sighed the saddest sigh of his life.

Every band of tribesmen — every last one — had returned empty-handed. How could this possibly be? Many, many islands had been searched upon and yet not a single one of those elusive and exotic maidens had been found! Apparently, those stories which Jia-banu had told him were just that — stories. Now how was he ever again to know the deepest and most splendid realms of passion if he could not obtain one single new and exotic mistress?

He sighed again. No doubt, this sad outcome was the decision of the God of Man-Joy. For whatever mysteriously incomprehensible reason, he was being punished. If only he knew why! Was it perhaps as retribution for his being a man of such deep and nearly continual carnal longings as he? Perhaps. But whatever the cause, this was certainly the darkest night of his life. To think that he, King Palawani, ruler of all Tiazanu, might never be allowed again to expel his kingly seed! It was almost too crushing a thought to bear.

In this state, even his impending summoning of the God of Death-Lava, by which to teach his failed tribesmen a lesson, offered little chance of boosting his spirits.

He sighed once again. It was nearly time for Kili-anu's evening servicing. Certainly, he would reach no release, but Kili-anu was, indeed, his favorite and the pleasure she brought him, though no longer sufficient, was nonetheless exquisite.

He picked up his conch shell to summon her.

But he never blew.

For just at that moment, two soft, gentle hands swept around him from behind and wrapped themselves delicately around his eyes.

Next, he felt firm breasts sliding deliciously across his back.

Then a sweet, seductive, and familiar voice spoke softly into his ear.

"Wanini pulu ho-hopu." *I am here, My King*, Kili-anu said. "I am here for you." Another swipe of her breasts across his back. "For you and nobody else but you. And I am most pleased to tell My King that I have a surprise for him."

King Palawani smiled. *This, I like.* "And what is this surprise, my little mistress?"

"It is, in truth, many surprises. And I have high hopes that My King will enjoy them."

With that, Kili-anu released her hands from his eyes and came around to stand before him.

He gasped. Her hair! It was no longer straight. Instead, it swirled about her head in sensual spirals, enticing curls, and ravishing loops, all held in place by dozens of small colorful jewels which reflected the moonlight a hundred-fold. It lent her a look that was as beautiful as it was exotic as it was arousing.

Indeed, it rendered her into the most beautiful woman he'd ever seen!

But then his gaze moved lower and he frowned. She was not unclothed, as was his preference. He looked down disapprovingly at the many gossamer silken layers that covered her lithe and slender body.

"You do not approve, My King," Kili-anu asked, tilting her head demurely, her voice growing less deferring and ever more seductive.

"You know that I prefer to view my mistresses as they were delivered to the world by the God of New-Life," he said, his voice stern, yet his eyes strangely intrigued by the enticing look that her coverings provided her.

She raised her hands above her head, clasping one within the other in an upward fluttering motion, and began to sway her hips — slowly, seductively. The fabric about her waist and hips was embedded with even more jewels and her movements dazzled him with twinkling reflected torchlight and moonlight—twinkling that followed her every move.

He leaned forward ever so slightly, his tongue grazing his upper lip.

"Oh, my," Kili-anu said. "If that be so, I should hasten to remove these garments for My King."

She slipped a white veil from her shoulders. It dropped soundlessly to the ground. Next, one in red. Then one in gold. And as she did, she continued to dance and sway and spin slowly around.

King Palawani gaped at her, transfixed. His eyes burned into her as her sweet shape became ever more revealed to him.

More veils came.

Then still more.

Mmm, this was most lovely, he thought, noting with some surprise, the rapid and thorough stiffening of his Royal Man-Muscle.

Finally, he could see that only one layer remained, for her dusky nipples were now visible. He dropped his gaze to the juncture of her thighs, but, oddly, found no hint of her dark womanly triangle showing through the fabric.

He held his breath, becoming increasingly anxious to view the removal of the final veil.

But, suddenly, she stopped. Then, slowly as can be, she stepped forward, coming to stand directly before him, her lithe torso inches from his face.

"It is a lovely silk," she whispered. "Perhaps My King should like to feel me through this final fabric before it is removed…"

He smiled, then reached out and grazed his fingers across her center.

And a sensation as powerful as a volcanic eruption shot through him. His Royal King-Thing sprang outward beneath his palm skirt. That touch! Silk and woman. Smooth and soft with no boundary between the two! He had never felt anything quite like it. Always, his mistresses were unclothed when in his presence. But this was something new altogether, something so inexplicably tantalizing. It was, indeed, most inexplicable, for why should a covered female body be more alluring than an uncovered one?

Whatever the reason, it was so. Being unable to see her skin somehow made her skin all the more alluring.

And now, of course, he wanted more.

He brought his hand lower, then gasped again. There was no hair to be felt! None at all!

"What have you done, my mistress?" he whispered huskily.

"This," Kili-anu answered. She raised her robe, tortuously slowly, up her legs. Palawani's gaze locked onto the hem as each new tiny portion of her thighs were bared to him. So strange, he thought, for he'd seen every inch of her countless times. And yet, *not* seeing these inches, save for one by one, was even more arousing.

Then…he saw.

Another gasp. Another collage of twitches below.

"Oh…" he breathed, quite un-king-like. "Oh…my…"

"I present you with my womanly parts," Kili-anu announced quietly. "So smooth now and unhidden. For the sole pleasure of My King."

Palawani's mouth was open so wide that a mango could very well have passed between his lips. "In the name of all the gods!"

Smiling coyly, Kili-anu continued to raise the robe over her stomach, her breasts, then her head.

Palawani gasped again. This was incomprehensible. How could this one view of her possibly be a thousand times more arousing than all the others?

He suddenly realized that he couldn't wait to discover what she intended to do for him next!

It wasn't at all what he'd thought.

Kili-anu smiled a most bewitching smile — a smile which, for the first time, displayed her teeth. She walked to his side, brushing her hip firmly against his shoulder, as would an equal have done, then picked up his conch shell and blew once.

In seconds, three tribesmen arrived. Two carried a long, narrow bamboo table, covered in silk. One carried a tray that held several flasks. They placed the table before the king and the tray at one end. Then they bowed and left.

"What…" Palawani couldn't stop the grin from curling the ends of his lips. "What are you planning to do next, my mistress?"

Kili-anu's look turned briefly serious. She looked him in the eye and she shook her head. "The others are your 'mistresses'. *My* name is Kili-anu and I would prefer that My King begin using it. Second, I'm afraid My King is mistaken. You see, I plan to do nothing…nothing, that is, except to lie down upon this table."

And she did.

Palawani's look turned disapproving once again, even angry.

"Nothing? What, then, are you —?"

"I have decided that it is My King who will be doing something for *me* for a change," she announced. "I have serviced you for many weeks, My King. Now it is *you* who will service me!" Again, she displayed her teeth. "Change is good, is it not?"

"*What*?" Palawani was bristling and he stared wide-eyed at this most audacious girl. "Do you realize that you risk a summons from the God of Death-Lava for such behavior?" Certainly, he would never consider such a thing. Still, the intrepid young woman needed to be put in her place.

Did she not?

Kili-anu smiled. "Oh, I do not think that this is in My King's best interest. You see, I have many oils here." She gestured the flasks, then selected one and held it out to her King.

"I'm warning you, my mistress..." he began as he took the flask from her.

"It is Kili-anu!" She then lay back and stretched her arms above her head. "Perhaps My King would enjoy administering these sensual, fragrant oils upon my young, warm, and nubile body. You see, I should like a massage and I am quite certain that you would greatly enjoy serving me with one. Perhaps My King would gladly indulge this one request...if it were to mean that he would thus have the privilege of stroking these oils upon me—everywhere—upon and perhaps even within my beautiful little body." She tilted her head coyly. "I am most certain that your hands will be delighted."

"Well, I—"

"I'm so soft, so young, and so tight, My King. Come...indulge in the sensation of my firm, oiled breasts gliding beneath your kingly cock. Anticipate the glorious feeling of my slippery and small behind. Then there are my nimble thighs... and...and much more."

"Well, I—"

"Then, of course, I would happily repay him by administering *his* massage. I would happily bring these oils upon his body and thoroughly prepare him for a night of passion, which, I promise, will be like no other."

King Palawani took some of the warm, fragrant oil upon his hands. Then, moving hesitantly, as if he'd never touched a woman before, he brought his hands upon her delightfully firm little thighs. Gently, he eased the oil into her skin in small, tentative circles, moving between her legs and close to her naked sex. She answered him with a shockingly loud wail of rapture which, praise the gods, was the most provocative sound he'd ever heard.

But then, the assertive little creature pulled his hands away from her center. "Not yet, My King. You must wait. Good things come to those who wait." As she spoke, she brought his hands up to her chest. "Here. Experience these first. And take your time. Savor them. We have all night. *I* shall inform you as to when my legs will open for you."

Palawani's growl quickly silenced has he began to rub and squeeze the oil softly into Kili-anu's ripe and wonderful breasts. "So, my bold and courageous little maiden," he said as he squeezed, "whatever has brought about this change in you?"

She smiled a very different smile. It was not seductive; it was not deferring. It was a wide, warm, and welcoming smile that King Palawani could not ignore in a thousand journeys around the Life-Star. "Upon the putting to sea of your — *ooh* — your expedition to find an exotic new maiden, I received a summons from Jia-banu. She — *aah* — confided in me her doubts that such a maiden would truly be found and so took me under her wing to school me in the supposed and mysterious ways of these bold and skillful women from the — *mmm* — many legends she has heard — *oh!*"

The king was most surprised. "*Did* she now?" As he spoke, his very slippery hands moved down to Kili-anu's stomach, where he discovered even more never-before-experienced sensations.

Kili-anu immediately took his hands and returned them to her breasts. "Not yet, you naughty boy." Then: "Oh, yes. Jia-banu taught me many practices which are sure to delight My King as he has never been delighted before!"

He was more than intrigued. "Such as?"

"Such as this…" Reaching down to her side, Kili-anu brought her oiled hand swiftly beneath his skirt where she grabbed his Royal Knee-Knocker daringly and hard, squeezed it, fingered it, and then moved beneath it where she did the same thing to his other parts…wantonly, powerfully, and so very skillfully.

He very nearly fell over from the delicious shock.

"That is…most stimulating, my maiden," he acknowledged between labored breaths. "But perhaps you should refrain for now, lest we risk too early a visit from the God of Man-Joy."

"As you wish, My King." Then: "My hips now, if you please."

The king did as he was told, now nearly delirious from pleasure at the mere touch of her curve. He caressed her there for a moment, then reached for more oil. Upon the return of his hands upon her hips, he said, "I am curious, my mistress — that is to say, Kili-anu — did Jia-banu summon you and you alone?"

Kili-anu nodded. "She did."

"And can you tell me why?"

"Certainly. She told me that you have indicated to her on more than one occasion that I am your secret favored one and that I alone should be the one to provide these exotic new services to My King. I took her tutelage to hear — with all my heart — for I am most fond of My King, I have…feelings for him, and providing him pleasure is not only my duty, but it is of utmost importance to me as well."

With her words, a surge of euphoria swept through King Palawani's being. It was warm and soothing and it left him speechless.

She is most fond of me?

Kili-anu smiled again as he continued with her massage. His hands were suddenly unsteady, even as he found himself falling into an almost trancelike state. His impatience was ever-growing, yet he found the wait strangely mesmerizing — especially for a man unaccustomed to waiting for anything. This, combined with the intoxicating aroma of the oil and the intoxicating vision of his beautiful little Kili-anu lying beneath his grasp, was having the most wondrous and hypnotic affect upon him. He was now so delirious that even time now passed beneath his awareness. Kili-anu's next action and words brought him back to the present.

She suddenly raised her knees and opened her legs to him. "Pray, do not forget my sweet little...um...oh, yes: my sweet little *pussy*, darling," she instructed in her most suggestive voice yet.

Palawani laughed jovially and long. "Pussy? *Pussy?* Oh, my...my...!"

Then, as he brought his oiled hands upon her naked sex, where they proceeded to delight both him and his Kili-anu, King Palawani made a mental note not only to cancel his tribesmen's appointment with the God of Death-Lava, but, rather, to reward them with a night of services with his five other concubines. He would not be needing them anymore and, indeed, had these men *not* failed to provide him with an exotic new mistress from afar, he might well have missed out on this most wondrous treasure — one which had been here, waiting for him, all along.

CHAPTER THIRTEEN

Meanwhile, in the Powell hut…

Mrs. Powell had just finished putting on her white satin nightgown. Then she looked over at her husband as he lay upon his twin bed, his mind clearly elsewhere. From the look on his face, she knew perfectly well what he was thinking about, or, rather, who: Someone tall, buxom, red-haired, nude, and wanton.

"Preston?" her voice was soft and gentle.

He blinked back to reality. "Hm? Yes, Sweetey?"

"Do you still find me attractive?"

He was clearly taken by her question. "Why, of course, I do, darling. You're Mrs. Preston Powell the Third! Of course, you're attractive. You're very attractive. I would have settled for no less."

"Thank you." She paused. "Am I beautiful?"

Her husband sat up in his bed, now looking quite concerned. "Why, of course, you are, darling.

Still as beautiful as on the day we were merged — er, that is to say, married."

She paused. "Then may I ask why you never make love to me anymore?"

His look of concern changed immediately to surprise. He pondered her question briefly. "Well, after all, Sweetey, people of our age simply don't engage in such youthful activities…" He paused and cocked his head. "Do they?"

"Preston, darling, we are not decrepit. Furthermore, if those looks you've given Gina as of late are any indication, it is clear that you still have thoughts that stray in that very direction."

"Well, I—"

"Preston…" Her look grew more serious. "I want you to make love to me as you once did. And I promise that I will withhold no favors."

"Sweetey! Why, I'm aghast! After all, what if anyone were to hear?"

Just then, the sound of Gina squealing wildly from somewhere in the jungle, broke through the night.

Sweetey and Preston turned their heads toward the sound and shook their heads in unison.

She pointed toward the window. "After *all* of the many sounds of lust and romance we've heard these past two days, I should think that our, I'm sure, more restrained noises would be of no concern to anyone else whatsoever, as they all seem *quite* wrapped up in their own, shall I say, affairs,"

Preston was thoughtful. "Well, I...I just don't know..."

She walked over beside his bed and sat down beside him. Such a handsome man, she thought. Handsome and gracious. After all these years, still, she loved him so much. She took his hand in hers, stroked his fingers, then laid it upon her thigh.

"Preston?" Her voice was soft and without a trace of her usual upper-class air. "Do you remember how you used to rub and caress my legs when we were younger? How I would lie against your chest, with my legs over yours, on the deck of your yacht, and you would run your hands over my knees and thighs for hours on end...like this..." She brought his now-trembling hand up and down the entire length of her thigh. "And beneath my dress...like this..."

She raised the hem of her nightgown up to her knees, then took his hand up beneath the satin fabric and moved it upon her thigh, swirling it higher and higher. His hand trembled for a moment longer...then relaxed...and then took on a will of its own, exploring her skin as if for the first time.

"Mmm...that's nice, darling," she murmured, smiling, savoring the multitude of long-lost tingles. "So very nice. Don't you agree?"

"Yes...yes, in fact, it is," he agreed, the usual air of upper-class in his voice gone as well. "It still feels so soft and smooth…like it used to."

She gave a quiet laugh. "Nearly so, perhaps." Then: "Do you know what I wish right now?"

"What's that, my dear?" he inquired just a bit cautiously as his hand continued to explore.

"I do wish that our butler was here. You see, if Rodney were here right now, we could have him move this nightstand aside and then push our two beds together the way they should be." She smiled her most beautiful and suggestive smile. "Now, wouldn't that be lovely?"

Suddenly, Preston smiled back at her, sat up, and pulled her into his arms. He kissed her tenderly. Then, pushing a wisp of her hair back behind her ear, he said, "Who needs a butler when you have a very capable and very willing 'man about the hut' right here — one who will happily tend to your every need and grant your every request!"

Mrs. Powell leaned down and kissed her husband deeply and long…just as she remembered doing all too many years ago.

* * * *

The cozy little beach was now lit aglow, the stars bright and the moon hunched just above the tops of the palm trees, but the Doc and Mary Lynn still lay side by side, he upon the cool sand, she upon her red gingham dress. Hours had passed since their chance encounter and yet they still had not moved beyond kissing and caressing. More than once Mary Lynn had whispered into his ear, "I want to make love to you, Doc, I so want to. I'm just nervous."

And each time he'd answered with the words: "Shh, it's okay, Mary Lynn. I'm happy just to be with you. Whatever unfolds…I'm happy."

Indeed, he was. Deliriously happy. Mary Lynn truly was the woman of his dreams. Never could he have imagined a woman so beautiful, so enticing, and so sweet. He couldn't seem to get enough of just gliding his fingers over the idyllic landscape of her body. It amazed him how he could touch or caress the same swell of the same unimaginably firm breast for seemingly unending moments and not grow bored. It fascinated him that such an innocuous thing as her shoulder could hold him spellbound. It astounded him that a single calf could appear to him as a thing of wonder.

But then he reminded himself that this was *Mary Lynn*! Her skin was, indeed, like magic. Her exquisite curvature, like a drug. Her beauty, simply all-consuming. It really was no wonder that he could remain so deeply entranced by her that he could very well have looked and touched forever.

And now, here he was, touching and exploring all the places he'd gazed upon so many times in recent days—in truth, since he'd known her—that they seemed to have taken on almost larger-than-life dimensions. All that wondering, all that longing, all that admiring was now right here, right now. This was Mary Lynn—beautiful Mary Lynn—and she was right here...with him.

Just then, she drew her mouth from his but kept her face barely an inch from his. Her eyes and her warm sweet breath continued to dazzle him.

"I'm a virgin, Doc."

He nodded, but refrained from pointing out that he'd always assumed that. Instead, he kissed her lightly on the forehead and waited.

She bit her lip. "And...I'm nervous. I truthfully don't know what to do or how to do it."

"Mary Lynn—"

"I want to make love with you so badly, Doc. I've dreamt about it for so long. But I'm..." She closed her eyes and softened her voice to a whisper. "I'm just so scared."

"Then we won't."

She smiled and shook her head. "What a sweet man you are." She kissed his lips gently and lingeringly. "I didn't say I was unwilling—just scared." Now she pressed her hand against his chest. "Could we just...go slow?"

He nodded and smiled. "Of course, Mary Lynn. I'm just as inexperienced as you—well, very nearly so. And just as afraid. Afraid of not pleasing you. Nervous about doing the wrong thing."

"I don't think that's possible. I mean..." She gazed at the moonlit beauty surrounding them. "Look at this! We have the ocean and the sand, the palm trees and the moon, the stars and the balmy breeze. We have the evening and we have each other. This is all so *right*. And *you* are so right. There is no 'wrong' here. At all."

"I guess we'll learn together, okay?"

She nodded. "Okay." Her whisper was barely audible.

The Doc's hand continued to glide across the contour of her hip, down her thigh, then back again. Over and over he repeated the same journey, unable to take the next step.

What to do? What to do?

Long difficult minutes passed. The only sounds were that of the surf, the nocturnal jungle birds, and an occasional monkey. Tracing her hip; tracing her thigh. Wanting to...to...

Finally, he took in a long, shaky breath and kissed her mouth deeply, then her ear, then her neck.

But then...still more hesitation.

Damn it! He knew what he needed to do. He needed to shut that overactive brain of his off for a little while and just *do*. Whatever seemed right and felt right...for her...for him...he would simply do it. He would do it and simply enjoy it...come what may.

Without a second thought, he took her by the shoulders and rolled her onto her back.

Mary Lynn's eyes stared wide at the sky, reflecting the moonlight, betraying her apprehension. She opened and closed her eyes. She wet and rewet her lips. She curled and uncurled her toes. She shuddered briefly.

The Doc's hand moved upon her once again, this time in a slowly downward-moving spiral from the peaks of her breasts, down over her rising and falling stomach, down to her small gossamer triangle. He touched her there forever...adoring... savoring...

Afraid...

But then, after looking into her eyes once more for reassurance, he gently raised her knees.

She took a deep breath, closed her eyes, and slowly spread them apart for him.

He gazed in awe at her sex, lit softly by the moonglow. Her womanly lips were so small. He hesitated still again, shaking his head ever so slightly. He couldn't possibly...

"Yes, Doc," came her whispered reassurance. "I—I'm ready."

He smiled faintly and nodded.

Then, positioning himself between her legs, he brought his tongue to their juncture.

At first, he simply kissed with gentle, lingering, exploring kisses. Then, with tentative strokes of his tongue across her outer lips that made her gasp and brought her bottom off the ground. He placed his hands beneath her to at last hold and behold her indescribably soft and supple cheeks. She eased herself back down upon his grasp and The Doc felt a wellspring of euphoria surge through him at what was truly the most incredibly wondrous sensation he ever could have imagined.

Then, with utmost care and gentleness, he slipped his tongue inside her.

In response to this second gasp came a sensual, masculine murmur from within him. Mary Lynn's innocence—her "girl next door" allure, now manifested in passion—thrilled him beyond measure.

He ventured deeper, delighting in the mingling of their wetness.

"Oh, Doc," she whispered, flinching in rapture to his every gentle thrust and slide against her sweet virgin tissues.

He then brought his tongue up to her tiny bud. Bathed it. Teased it. Suckled it. Pulled it as gently as a butterfly within his lips. Held it. Claimed it.

"Oh, Doc! Oh, my...my...oh, Doc!"

Mary Lynn's first orgasm was music to his soul. She gasped and gasped. She bucked and wracked her body. Her thighs squeezed hard around him. Her womanly wetness flowed. Every syllable of her erotic delight was called out to the night.

And then, she lay still once again as he continued to pleasure her.

And all the while, he delighted in her. His tongue delighted in the taste of her — so sweet and mild. His eyes delighted in the shape of her — so tight and curvaceous. His hands delighted in gently squeezing that glorious behind of hers in wonder — the feeling so impossibly smooth, so indescribably perfect. And his ears delighted in the sound of her gasps, murmurs, and moans — so innocent and infectious.

The more he took in all of Mary Lynn's charms, the more he wanted her. God, he wanted her! But he didn't want to rush her. And he didn't want to hurt her. He simply continued to move his lips and tongue upon and within her, bathing her, lubricating her as much as he possibly could. He used one finger — then two — very, very slowly, gently, and respectfully, hoping to relax her inner muscles and widen her virgin passage. Gently, he eased them in and out of her, pushing just a bit deeper each time, delighting in the titillating grip of her warm, moist flesh.

No, he would not hurry her.

Or…was it he himself who he didn't want to hurry?

A moment later he felt her spreading her legs wider. And wider still.

Then he felt her hands on his shoulders.

Then he heard her say, "I'm ready, Doc. I'm ready for you. I want you inside me. But please..."

"I will go slow," he finished for her.

He brought himself onto his elbows atop her and looked deep into her trusting wide-open eyes...

Then he reached down, and guided himself inside her, slow as the shadow of a sundial.

God, she was tight! So impossibly tight. He had to be hurting her.

He paused. He dared not move until he felt the slightest sensation of her relaxing. Then he moved again, as slowly as he possibly could, allowing each stroke to venture ever deeper, one daring and overwhelming millimeter at a time.

He was keenly aware of the sensation of every taut fold of her that soon surrounded his length.

He began to kiss her soft, shapely lips as he moved, his mind in utter disbelief. If someone had said to him, even one day before, that on this night, he would be lying on a moonlit tropical beach, making love to this woman, he would have deemed that person certifiably insane. It was simply too incomprehensible, even for a man so accustomed to comprehending just about everything, that this could possibly be happening to him.

Here he was, making love to Mary Lynn Saunders! It was he who had been granted this overwhelming experience before all other men. It was he whose body was now melded upon and enmeshed within hers. It was he who was at last feeling passion and physical euphoria such that he could never have known—and with the one woman on earth who could do that for him.

"Oh…Doc," she whispered again. "I could never…have imagined…I could never in a million years have…" She shook her head in disbelief as her words trailed off.

Then she smiled.

Then she gasped.

Then she moaned softly.

"Never…ever…" he began, his voice trailing off as he too, looked upon her in disbelief.

She nodded.

No further words were necessary.

Instead, he brought his lips to hers again and they began to kiss their most passionate kiss. It was all tongue and teeth and lips. Their mouths were so wet. He plunged his tongue deep and hard, desperate to know her this way. Soft sounds emanated from her throat—or was it his? Their mouths moved wildly against one other, as if making up for the three years that they could never get back.

Their breaths quickened and grew louder as their two bodies continued to unify.

But then, after long, yet very brief moments, he slowed. The sensations were beginning to overtake him and he didn't want the experience to end too soon for either of them. He wanted the warm, liquid feeling of gliding within her to continue and continue and continue. He wanted to behold her seductive wide-open mouth throughout the night. He wanted to feel the skin of her entire length against his forever.

But it was no use, for at that moment Mary Lynn began to move faster, pulling him deeper inside her, then softly thrusting her body against his. And her moans grew louder. And her head thrashed more wildly upon the cool sand.

And her second orgasm overcame the two of them.

He couldn't hold on. Her face was just too beautiful. Her sex was just too soft and too tight. And this night was just too perfect. He was overpowered. He was overwhelmed. And he was overcome with ecstasy.

There was to be no turning back now. It was all around him now.

The tide was coming in. They were now just a few feet from the water and the froth was just beginning to reach their bodies, adding enticing shudders to the myriad sensations that continued on their upward spiral to overtake him.

When the Doc reached his climax, he immediately knew that this was nothing like the night before. With Gina, his attention had focused tightly upon his sex and her sex—upon those few entwined inches of male and female and nothing more. This—*this*—was all that and more. So much more. This was everything and it was everywhere. It flowed throughout his entire being and into his soul. It was heat and lust, softness and innocence, romance and magic, man and woman.

And then…there was just the sea.

And the moon.

And the sand.

He lay down beside her once again, his hand gliding across her hip once again. They smiled at each other. Then, in tandem, they turned their bodies toward the sea, allowing the spray to cool them.

Not two mesmerizing moments later, the next miracle arrived.

"I love you," she whispered.

Her eyes were nearly touching his as she spoke the three words which he knew would, in some way or another, change his life forever.

His response was immediate, for her affirmation meant the end to any remaining uncertainty within him. "And I love you, Mary Lynn. I *love* you. And I'm joyful, grateful, and proud to say it."

She smiled. "Do you think that maybe we have for quite some time now?"

He smiled back. "Oh, I think that 'we' have known this for far longer than that. I may be a scientist and thus not one for talking about things of a non-material nature. But I am also a disciple of the late, great Albert Einstein, a man who understood the power and mystery of the Universe far more deeply and completely than I. He knew — and I've come to know — that nothing happens by accident. And that includes us."

She looked at him, not fully comprehending.

"Don't you see, Mary Lynn? The Universe put us on that boat together for a reason! And that reason was so that our love, borne of non-material potentiality, could, on this very night, manifest into reality. Love is the most powerful force in the Universe and, as such, many, many courses of fate have been orchestrated by Universal decree, as it were, to allow this very love of ours to unfold.

"Ah," she replied, smiling and shaking her head in what appeared to be amazement.

He smiled warmly. "This was, in the truest sense of the word, *meant to be*."

"I don't need a scientist to figure that out for me," Mary Lynn replied with a wide smile, just before claiming his lips and mouth in their deepest kiss yet.

The first of many.

Then, much later: "Doc? Can I ask you something?"

He paused his exploration of her ear and looked at her. "Of course, you can."

"Why does everyone call you 'Doc' all the time?"

"Pardon?"

She smiled. "Well, I've often wondered how it came to be that we all just started calling you 'Doc' when you have a perfectly good name: Ray."

He laughed softly. "You know something? It has been so long since I've been called 'Ray' that even I have begun to forget my own given name. Hearing you say it just now made me think, for a brief instant, that you were talking about someone else!"

They laughed softly. Then Mary Lynn pressed her soft, soft lips against his. "I think I'm going to call you Ray from now, if that's okay."

He smiled warmly. "I actually like hearing it."

"Good. I'll do that—at least when we're alone."

The Doc smiled broadly. "Well, in that case, I should think that I'll be hearing it for countless times to come!"

* * * *

Later that night, while snoring in his hammock, Finnegan was roused from sleep by faint moans and a rustling sound from below. It didn't take him long to realize that the Captain was at it again: stroking his little ding-dong right there in his hammock.

He turned his head toward the sound.

"So…which one are you thinking about this time?"

The Captain moaned once again, then laughed softly. "Little buddy, that could perhaps be the stupidest question you've ever asked."

"Just teasing." Finnegan yawned. "Nope, Cap, I don't think I need to ask that question ever again."

"That's right—you don't. In fact, I hereby order you not to ask that question again! And I certainly hope that I never have to ask *you* that question again either. Right?"

"Nope, never again, Cap, don't worry." Then: "And there's something else I don't think we have to wonder about anymore."

The Captain chuckled quietly. "You mean, who's better?"

"Mm-hm."

"No, siree. I mean, Mary Lynn will always have a special place in my heart. But when it comes to wanting a woman...it's Gina LaPlante, hands down."

"That's right, Cap: Hands-down. And elbows down. And bent down. And going down." Then, grinning: "Of course, Mary Lynn's *ass* will always have a special place in my heart, you know what I'm saying?"

Just then he yelped when he felt the sting of the Captain's hat as it shot up from below and caught him on the side of his head.

"You keep your dirty mind where it belongs, little buddy, y'got that? There's only one ass and one woman either one of us needs to think about from now on and I don't want you to ever forget that!"

"Yes, sir."

"Good. Now that we got that out of the way, shut up and go to sleep!"

Finnegan groaned reluctantly, then reached down to gently soothe his still-tender big buddy. "Aye, aye, sir. Good night. Oh, and sweet dreams."

"Oh, I'm sure they will be, Finnegan." The Captain yawned once again. "Sweet and then some!"

"Yeah," Finnegan replied, his voice dripping with testosterone, "sweet and then some!"

* * * *

Later still, the Doc was sitting at the table in his hut, just finishing his latest journal entry:

Yes, I have now come to the overwhelming realization that there are some realms in life where science is not the answer and, indeed, has no place. Rather that research the beauty and allure of women, I am hereby given over to enjoying these mysterious delights first-hand and living them with all my heart, mind, and body...with the woman of my dreams.

He might have written more, but just then the soft, sweet voice from his bunk on the other side of the hut stopped his pen in its tracks.

"Come to bed, Ray."

The End

ALSO BY J.C. CUMMINGS

Thank you so much for reading this book! I hope you enjoyed it and found it titillating!

Meanwhile, might I ask you to consider writing an honest review for this book? This will help me to continue writing the books I love best: erotic fiction! It will also help future readers to make informed decisions about which books to add to their collection. Please take a moment to return to the web site where you purchased this book and leave your review for others.

And, of course, spreading the word about this book to your friends would be *greatly* appreciated!

Thanks in advance and happy reading!

Also, as a thank-you for purchasing this book, just email me at **jc.tantalia@outlook.com** and put "book offer" in the subject line. I will send you a free PDF version of this story that uses the original character names. As per copyright law, I cannot sell this book with these names, but I can give it away. Of course, I will never, ever give away or sell your email address.

Below are many of my best offerings in adult fiction. Perhaps some of them will strike a chord within you! All are available at Amazon.com.

NAUGHTY MEN AT WORK Series

For your naughty reading pleasure...here are six short erotic tales of hot and not-so-ethical men who use their professional status and positions of authority in order to have their way with the hot and not-so-worldly female beauties who hire their services. These stories include domination and submission, steamy sex of all kinds, "sexploitation" of young and not-so-young women, frisking, fondling, fingering, and even a touch of scintillating romance. They are written to engage your fantasy-hungry mind and bring out the appreciation of naughtiness we all crave!

Book 1
My Very Naughty Piano Teacher

When gorgeous female students are lax in their practicing, they may find out that their sexy teacher's piano and bench have other non-musical uses…both painful and very pleasurable.

Book 2
My Very Naughty Therapist

When a touch-starved young woman comes to her hot new therapist for help, she receives a therapy session like none she's ever had before. Immersion therapy to the hilt.

Book 3
My Very Naughty Handyman

When a horny young woman sees her new handyman strut his gorgeous, well-muscled stuff into her home she embarks on a campaign of teasing, torment, and temptation that may ultimately go too far—even with a work-focused professional like the one she hired. A carpenter's sawhorse can, indeed, come in handy at times...

Book 4
My Very Naughty Designer

It's a good thing that her hot, new wardrobe designer is gay…otherwise the way he fondles and gropes her body with his hands and measuring tape might come off as highly unethical. But, boy, her new outfits sure are tempting…

Book 5
My Very Naughty Photographer

A camera-shy high school senior, just turned 18, finds out that posing can be fun — if it's for the right photographer — even if most of the pictures wind up more suited for a men's magazine than her school yearbook.

Book 6
My Very Naughty Doctor

Sue hates going to her gynecologist... more than most middle-aged women in fact. So, imagine her surprise when her next exam takes place in a college classroom of gawking and horny young interns and puts her quivering body through more embarrassment than any woman could possibly endure...and ultimately more ecstasy!

Five-book bundle
PROFESSIONAL PERVERTS Series

Here are five stories about men who use their positions of power in order to have their way with five beautiful and innocent women! I had a blast writing them and they are just dripping with kind of hands-on debauchery most men fantasize about (but would likely never admit to their lady friends)!

Book 1
Boss' Orders
When Angela Martin is hired by Guardian Trust, one of the largest banking/investment companies in the world, she's thrilled about the shockingly high salary she's been offered. But when she meets the company CEO, Derek Michaels, for the first time she comes to learn two things very quickly: 1) That her work for the company includes her offering herself to its executives and clients in any manner they wish, and 2) That she will follow her boss' orders immediately and without question. Michaels decides to "train" her, right then and there, with a session of what can only be described as: the world's sleaziest, most degrading and humiliating game of "Simon Says" ever. He follows this up with additional training in the art of submission, compliance, and much more!

Book 2
Doctor for a Day
Attorney Nate Bishop is an ass-addict of the highest order. He craves curvy female rear ends the way a banker craves foreclosures. And it has been his life's dream to give a beautiful bottom a feeling-up it would never forget. So, when his friend, a doctor, calls in desperate need of his legal services, Nate offers to take his case for free — with the stipulation

that he be allowed to pose as a doctor, at his office, and probe his most gorgeous patient, Becky. Becky, Nate has been told, was blessed with the most beautiful bottom known to man and this sleazy attorney would like nothing more than to get his hands on—and his fingers in—this adorable creature's caboose. In the end, Nate is treated to the dream of a lifetime: Becky's bountiful behind…but not without having the tables—exam tables, that is—turned on him!

Book 3
The Lawyer, the Virgin and the Strip Search

Sweet and curvy Kelli Green finds herself at the office of attorney Sam Archer. She's seeking help in bringing to justice a sleazy border guard who had performed an unethical cavity search on her. Little does she know that Sam Archer is, in fact, a bigger pervert than the border guard!

Book 4
The Doctor's Twin Brother

Drop-out and lifelong loser, Mick Sloan, is so ever-loving jealous of his super-successful brother, Prescott, that he just can't stand it. Prescott is an Army doctor who spends his days giving gyno exams to nubile young female recruits. Mick, a pervert since kindergarten, would, of course, like nothing better than to have a chance to do the very same thing! So, he devises a clever but nasty scheme where he locks Prescott out of action for a while, steals his uniform, and arrives at the base ready, willing, and able to feel, fondle, and finger one young hottie after another. Only, of course, if things go according to Mick's plan. Perhaps, in the end, they just may go better!

Book 5
The Unpaid Mechanic
In this fun and nasty tale, Jesse, an auto mechanic who has just come in to a whole lot of money, decides to begin offering his services for free...but only to the most gorgeous female customers. In exchange for top-quality mechanic work — and a few other perks — he gets them, well, atop the hood of his Lamborghini and finds himself living out the ultimate car-lover's and lady-lover's fantasy. That is, until a rich and beautiful but very cold-hearted hottie shows up with quite possibly the world's greatest car in need of Jesse's expert hands. But with a woman as mean-spirited as this one, are even her abundant female charms enough to make him take the gig?

Bartering for Booty
My newest novella! Hot and good-hearted Melanie Sweetwater has made a career out of offering herself and her grabbable goodies for anything she finds herself in need of, be it school test answers, retail

discounts, professional services, anything! So when the home of her dreams comes on the market, a sleazy realtor, along with a few fellow lenders, offers it to her for a whopping discount — in exchange for a full day and night of any and all sexual favors they demand of her. Melanie is game…until she comes to realize just how "demanding" their demands happen to be. Now she learns the hard way that, when you barter for booty, the house always wins!

ABOUT THE AUTHOR

Hi! I am a happy, hard-working, and fun-loving author of erotic fiction living the seaside-cottage lifestyle in beautiful, sundrenched North Carolina. Ooh, I love my work! Sitting out on the deck, typing away at the sexploits of one randy couple after another (mmm!) ...and all the while feeling my own tingles from the sun and the ocean breeze on my skin, the rhythmic pounding of the surf in my ears, and view after view of semi-naked bodies spread out before me...well, I absolutely cannot think of anything I'd rather do more (for a living, anyway)!

People often ask me if my stories are products of my imagination or life experience. Of course I answer "both!" However, I must add that even if a story is conceived purely in my rather dirty mind, it never goes to publication before being "tested" in the laboratory of real life. I'm dead serious! For starters, it's a ton of fun and I love the texture and depth it gives to even my shortest tales.

Another question I'm often asked is: How did I come to be an author of erotic fiction? Well, when I was attending law school, one of my professors noticed right away that law was not a good fit for me. I admitted that I was here only to satisfy my parents' expectations. So he sat me down and said, "JC, the secret to a great career and a great life is to take all the things you love to do, find a way to merger them together, and make that your work."

So, I *un*-enrolled my cute little butt out of law school pronto and rolled the top three loves of my life together — writing stories (which I'd been doing since I was in middle-school), living by the ocean (which I longed to do since middle school), and sex (which I'd been doing since ...) — and here I am.

So that's how I became what I am. But I also must say that, in addition to the pleasure I get from writing stories, I get an absolute thrill from knowing that, somewhere in the world, someone like you is getting some pleasure and perhaps a bit of titillation from reading them. So I'm sure I'll be doing this for a long time to come!

Follow me on Twitter right here!
https://twitter.com/GilliganBabes

You can visit my Amazon Author Page at: **https://www.amazon.com/J.C.-Cummings/e/B00O75NLGY**

Email me at: **jc.tantalia@outlook.com** and let me know what you think about this story, or if you have any suggestions for future Gilligan's Island parodies. Thanks and I look forward to hearing from you!

Made in the USA
Columbia, SC
24 August 2021

44234623R00157